Midwives of Moses

JENIFER JENNINGS

Peacock Press
3040 Plantation Ridge Drive
Green Cove Springs, FL 32043

To those who give life and those who help protect it.

A Note to You

Dear Reader,

Writing about history can be tough. Following along as a reader can be even tougher. So, I wanted to add this note to offer an outline of this novel. Please take into consideration that because each person looking back at recorded history will measure dates and events in different ways, we'll never have a 100% accurate timeline. Also remember, this novel is a work of fiction. Though it is a story based on real people and real events it's, in and of itself, complete fiction.

It always amazed me that the Pharaohs' names are never mentioned in the Biblical account. To this day, scholars debated as to the exact rulers under which this story took place.

Pharaohs' rules were measured and recorded in years of their rule. They did not record birth and deaths or other events by the calendar year as you and I would today. Many Pharaohs also co-ruled which produced overlapping dates. In addition, Pharaohs took multiple wives. Though there was a wife hierarchy as to keep the line of rule clear.

Upon doing my own research, I've settled on the 18th Dynasty of Egypt as the setting for my fictitious retelling of this story. For the Pharaohs in this book, I'd like to give you an outline of my calculations of dates. After much research, and discovering that every historian has their own guesstimation about the years, this is my best guess.

Placing the cornerstone fact into place that the Exodus from Egypt by the Hebrews happened in 1446 B.C., that would put Moses' birth in 1526 B.C. since he was eighty when they left Egypt.

- Thutmose I = ruled 1529-1516
- Thutmose II = ruled 1516-1503
- Queen Hatshepsut/Pharaoh Hatshepsu = ruled 1503-1482
- Thutmose III = ruled 1482-1432

Regardless of which Pharaohs ruled, we do have the names of two Hebrew midwives, Shiphrah and Puah recorded. The men, who were considered earth dwelling gods, did not get the honor of having their names listed for record. Instead, that honor goes to two brave women who risked their own lives to spare the lives of hundreds, possibly thousands, of Hebrew male children.

Numbers 1:46 tells us that there was a recorded census counting 603,550 men over the age of 20 who left Egypt. Certainly, these midwives assisted in keeping some of them alive during Pharaoh's edict 80 years prior to them leaving Egypt.

God always rewards faith. This story is simply another shining example of what awaits those who trust God's way and put action to their faith. I'm proud to share their story with you in hopes that when you face a difficult circumstance, you'll remember these women and be brave enough to choose God's way.

If you'd like to read more stories about people of faith, check out jeniferjennings.com/books.

~Jenifer Jennings

Chapter 1

"And the king of Egypt spake to the Hebrew midwives, of which the name of the one was Shiphrah, and the name of the other Puah:"
-EXODUS 1:15

1526 B.C., Egypt

Puah's young arm muscles burned with strain. She was doing her best to help bear the weight of the pregnant woman who was in the final stages of labor. They had helped her squatted upon the birthing stones while Shiphrah knelt underneath her to catch the newborn baby. Puah and Rania stood on either side of the woman with a grip on each of her arms for support while she pushed. This was not the first time Puah had assisted with a birth, but it felt like it.

"Push, Leora!" Shiphrah shouted from beneath the pregnant woman.

Her mentor, Shiphrah, told Puah that with time her arms would build up strength. Apparently, three years had not been long enough. She adjusted her feet to spread the weight over her body like Shiphrah showed her. The movement helped.

She glanced over the pregnant woman's head to Rania, another midwife apprentice holding the woman's other arm. She must be struggling with the weight as well because her face was scrunched as if she was the one in labor. Her copper-toned skin was shifting to tones of red. She held her bottom lip between her teeth and her strict focus was on the woman between them.

The pregnant woman was a Hebrew not much older than the two of them. This was her first delivery and she had called for the best midwife in all Egypt, Shiphrah.

Puah had the great fortune to seek out mentorship under Shiphrah. She had just advanced her last two apprentices and was in search of fresh young girls to train. One Hebrew and one Egyptian. Puah had been the selected Hebrew and Rania was the Egyptian.

Shiphrah believed strongly in giving equal training to both groups of women. A practice most unheard of for either culture. Though both enjoyed living in the same land, they were not melded as one. Each remained distinct in almost every way from the other. Even after three hundred years, Puah's people held to their identity as God's chosen ones.

Being the youngest in a long line of girls, Puah knew her family wouldn't have the resources necessary to offer a lavish dowry for her. At the age of twelve, she sought out Shiphrah to train her as a midwife. At least she could put her hands to some kind of good service.

Puah looked down. She noticed drops of sweat on her mentor's wrinkled forehead. Her dark brown hair was also weighed down with dampness. She also noticed that her hands were too preoccupied with widening the pathway of delivery to wipe her own brow. Her burnt cinnamon eyes were transfixed on her task. Puah thought if a sandstorm had blown up in the room, she didn't think her mentor would even blink.

The young midwife in training glanced over at the pile of clean linens that Shiphrah had expertly stacked within reach. It crossed her mind to grab one and pat her mentor's forehead. The burning in her arms caught her breath. She feared if she released her grip even for a moment, the woman would topple on the birthing stones. Rania was of the same age and strength. She knew the girl could not bear the weight alone.

The pregnant woman grunted and bore down hard.

"That's right," the midwife encouraged. "Not much more now."

Shiphrah had delivered hundreds of babies. She made the duty of helping women bring new life into the world look as effortless as breathing.

"Each birth has its own challenges," the older woman had instructed on their walk to this delivery. "Be prepared for anything and everything."

Leora's scream brought Puah back to her task. She dared a peek between the woman's legs. She saw a dark-haired head slowly appear and then, just as easily disappear back inside its mother. She looked at Shiphrah with wide eyes.

"It'll drop back down," the mentor said without taking her focus off her task. "That's part of the process. It'll probably do that a few more times."

Puah watched her intense gaze on the opening.

"I've witnessed countless babies fight the birthing process," Shiphrah commented. "Many refuse to leave the warmth of their mother's womb. This little one is being extremely stubborn."

"Just…like…father…" the pregnant woman joked between labored breaths.

Puah chuckled.

"What happens next?" Rania asked from the other side of the pregnant woman.

For the first time in hours, Shiphrah reached over to the pile of cloths and wrapped a linen around her hand. "I don't care how strong you think you are," she said toward her two students. "Always, and I do mean always, wrap your hands with clean linens to catch a newborn. They are more slippery than a greased dog. The last thing you ever want do is have to explain to a mother, who is flooded with the strength of a lioness, that you just dropped her baby."

Leora groaned.

"One more big push should do it." Shiphrah glanced up. "Hang on, ladies."

The two young girls tightened their grip on the mother's arms to help keep her stable.

Another scream erupted from Leora's mouth.

"He's here," the midwife shouted with glee. She held up the shimmering, olive-toned wiggling boy.

"Praise God," Leora said as she collapsed into the arms of the two women helping support her body.

"Look at him," Puah said, still holding Leora's arm. "He's lovely."

"He sure is," Rania commented.

Her eyes watered. "That was so beautiful!"

"Life is beautiful," her mentor agreed as she cleaned the boy with a mixture of water and wine. "Babies come into the world at their own time, but they always make an impact."

She examined the baby while rubbing him down with oil and wrapped him in a fresh cloth. "Perfect," she reported. "He's absolutely perfect."

"Thank you." Leora grinned. She sighed with relief as the two apprentices helped her to a waiting pile of pillows.

The older midwife laid the boy on his mother's chest to enjoy his first meal.

"Another healthy Hebrew," Puah commented on their way out of the house and into the open streets of Avaris.

"It still amazes me every time I see a woman give birth," Rania said. "It's like they are immortals. To have that kind of strength when a human being is being ripped from your loins-"

"We don't rip anything from anyone," Shiphrah corrected.

"You know what I'm trying to say."

The older woman cut her eyes at her young student. "I do, but you must have a little more respect for your service."

"Of course."

"Where are we going next?" Puah asked.

"Into Memphis." Shiphrah moved swiftly past

several mud-brick buildings as they entered the main street of the Egyptian city. She slowed as the houses grew familiar and a whitewashed one stood proudly sparkling. "Ah, here we are."

The three women stopped at the entry gate so Shiphrah could knock.

A woman in a modest dress answered the door with a bow. Puah could tell right away she was a Hebrew. Some women worked as servants for their Egyptian counterparts. It was a good wage. It wasn't an ideal situation, but often times a necessary one.

"Greetings, Ziva. Is your mistress home?" Shiphrah asked.

It always amazed Puah at how easily the older woman could switch her speech from Hebrew to Egyptian and back again without missing a single word. She was sure it was only one of the countless reasons so many women called upon her.

"Yes." Ziva waved the women in. "This way."

As they were guided down a long entrance hall, Puah took note of each room they passed. Egyptians and Hebrews lived much differently. Each dressed and spoke distinctly, but it was entering a house in which one could really see the division.

The Hebrew home they had come from in Avaris was a small, square design. An open courtyard welcomed visitors. Wood pillars divided the other half of the house into usable rooms. The few rooms were used by every member of the family. There were no paintings or decorations to cover up the simple walls. Very few even contained furniture.

The house area was divided into two levels with an exposed rooftop. Homes were set close enough together that one could have a conversation with their neighbor while working on the roof.

The lavish Egyptian home stood more rectangular with a massive wall around the outside to close off unwanted guests. The main house held multiple rooms used for various activities such as sleeping, eating, and worship of the family's chosen deity. A second level was also separated for multiple uses, but it's top was closed off from the outside. Many were painted or had white limestone applied to the outside to keep the inside of the home cooler against the rays of the harsh sun.

Walls and floors of each room were covered with pictures and sculptures. Pastel colors livened up each room. Couches, tables, and storage vessels cluttered every corner. The simple Hebrew eye could easily get overwhelmed trying to take it all in. Puah blinked a few times to clear her vision.

As they exited the main house and made their way to the back of the property, she noticed the separate kitchen, well, stable, garden, and servant quarters. It was the kitchen where Ziva led them to her mistress.

"Greetings, Anta," Shiphrah offered when they found the woman of the house kneading dough on a flat piece of wood on the floor.

Puah noticed the recently caught waterfowl swinging from the ceiling. No doubt to be the main course of their evening meal. She could smell the fresh blood dripping from its body. It had been a while since she had tasted meat. To her people, meat was a rare delicacy. To an Egyptian, it was just another way to satisfy their hunger.

"Greetings, ladies." The woman wiped her hands on a towel and then placed it over the dough.

Ziva stood over her mistress and allowed Anta to wrap her arms around hers. With a cautious movement, she helped lift the woman from her seated position to her feet.

Anta was a beautifully radiant Egyptian woman. She wore a lily-white robe wrapped and tied to accentuate her curves but also allowed room for her rounded midsection to poke out. The red sash Puah had seen her wear on a number of occasions would normally hug her smaller waist and thereby be short enough to spare its material from the ground. With her belly expanded to hold her unborn child, she knotted it under her bulge so that it hung low enough to elegantly sweep the sandy floor as she walked.

Pieces of her dull hair stuck to her forehead

from under a shiny, black wig. A sign of wealth to any who wondered if the wearer were affluent enough to afford such extravagance.

Puah tucked some loose strands of her thick, russet hair back under her head covering. If she lived to be as old as Eve, she would probably never afford such luxuries.

Several gold necklaces jingled against Anta's neck collar as she embraced each midwife. "I'm happy you have come to see me." She handed each woman a small piece of bread sprinkled with salt.

Puah graciously accepted the friendship offering with a bright smile. It was nice to know some Egyptians still tried to befriend Hebrews even in shifting times.

The recent Pharaoh change three years prior had caused unease in the land of Goshen with the addition of taskmasters over the Hebrew people. It seemed the new Egyptian god on earth, Thutmose, was going to make a name for himself by expanding his borders at the same time as he was placing more control over the Hebrews.

She was glad she had chosen to be a midwife as soon as she was old enough to make the choice for herself. At least she would be spared the life of a house servant like many of her female friends.

She observed Ziva, who had stayed nearby waiting for her next orders. She wondered what led her to serve Anta and from which tribe she came from in Goshen. The woman stood as still as a statue, though her muscles were tense with anticipation of her next task. Bright onyx eyes were transfixed on her mistress.

Gazing around the large backyard, Puah wondered if any of the materials of the buildings had been forged by Hebrew hands. Many young husbands had been sent to hard work in the quarries to help expand the presence of Egyptian architecture in the land. Hebrews were always seen a little lower in Egyptian eyes, but it seemed the new royal family was forcing them to bow even lower.

She didn't have to worry about a husband. The life of a midwife was often solely focused on helping couples welcome life into the world. She understood that part of the calling and welcomed it. No one had caught her eye and she was sure she hadn't captured any man's attention.

She tried not to worry about the growing oppression either. She was a midwife. Or at least one in training. The guild was held in high regard for their skill in medicine and was considered one of very few groups that didn't have to fear being forced into slavery. They were too valuable to Egyptians to be placed under thumb.

As she chewed, the warm bread seasoned with cumin melted the salt into a divine sensation in her mouth. The hefty scent of stew wafted through the air. Her mouth watered over the salt and delicious aromas. It was the tastes of Egypt that made her heart long to live as they did.

"Oh?" Shiphrah said over the bite in her mouth. She motioned to the woman's stomach. "Is anything wrong?"

"I'm not sure." Anta rubbed her belly. "I don't think it's anything to worry about."

"She has not been feeling well the past few days," Ziva offered. "She complains of pain."

Anta glared at her servant who ducked her head.

"Forgive me for speaking without permission," she whispered from under her warm brown locks. "I'm simply worried about you."

The mistress softened. "Why don't you go pick some fruit for tonight?"

Ziva bowed, grabbed a basket, and left the kitchen.

" 'Get a Hebrew servant,' " Anta repeated the words of her husband with mockery. " 'They're hard workers,' he said. At least an Egyptian maid would know when to hold her tongue."

"So," Shiphrah said quickly changing the subject. "What's this about pain?"

"It comes and goes." The pregnant woman rubbed her belly again. "Worse when I eat or try to sleep."

"Still feeling the baby kick?"

She looked down at her freshly woven sandals.

Shiphrah exchanged a glance with her two apprentices before returning her gaze to the woman in front of her. "Anta?"

"Less the last two days," she whimpered without raising her head.

"I see," she said. "Let's have a look at you."

Puah and Rania helped the woman into the house and positioned her on one of the couches so Shiphrah could examine her.

After a few moments, the mentor motioned for the two girls to follow her to the next room. "We'll be right back," she called over her shoulder. "Just rest."

"What is it?" Rania asked when they were a safe distance away to speak freely. "You look worried."

"I am," Shiphrah shared honestly. "I think we need to try to encourage delivery."

"Now?" Puah wondered. "How close is she?"

"Close enough that we're not in any real danger, but I'm afraid the baby might be in trouble. Without any way to know for sure, it's a tough choice."

"What are you going to tell her?" Rania asked.

"The truth." The mentor squared her shoulders. "Every woman deserves that much."

The three returned to Anta's side.

"I'm going to tell you something." Shiphrah hesitated. "But I don't wish to frighten you."

"The baby?" Anta clutched her mid-section.

"I believe the baby might be in trouble. If the baby is moving less, it might mean something is wrong. Especially if you're having pain."

"Or?" Anta raised an eyebrow.

"Or…" She sighed. "It could be nothing. Your body might just be preparing for delivery. Every woman is different."

"So, nothing could be wrong?"

"It's possible."

Anta thought for a moment. "But you don't think so."

"I think we should try to help the baby come quicker. You're far enough along now. If something is wrong, I can help once the baby is here. If the baby stays inside and we can't help…" She spread out her palms.

"I see."

"We'll be here to help," Puah offered with a pat on the woman's hand.

Rania nodded in agreement. "Right here with you."

"How long will Ziva be gone?" Shiphrah asked retrieving the bag she had left at the front door.

"Oh, she didn't go far. She hasn't in the last few days."

"She's worried about you too," Puah said.

"I know." A pain caused her to tense. "I should have listened when she wanted to call on you days ago."

"Yes," Shiphrah agreed. "You should have. Now, let's prepare for a baby."

She gave instructions to her students to set up

the birthing stones while she prepared her mixtures and cloths.

Hours into the night, Anta squatted upon the cool stones, panting, "How much longer?"

"Hard to tell," Shiphrah called from beneath her.

"Stay strong," Puah said with a tightened grasp on the woman's arm.

"You're doing well," Rania added.

"I don't know how much longer I can keep it up."

"Let's try another big push," the older midwife instructed.

"I don't know."

"Here." Puah wiped Anta's brow with a wet rag. "We are all right here with you."

"Push now," Shiphrah urged.

Anta bore down so hard her face turned red.

"That's it. Almost—Oh! Stop! Stop pushing."

She released her breath. "What's wrong?"

"I see the problem." Shiphrah's forehead scrunched in concentration. "Hold perfectly still."

"What's wrong with my baby?"

"Almost got it. Don't push."

Several moments of agonizing silence hung between the women.

"Well?" Anta demanded.

"The cord is around the neck." She attempted again to get her fingers between the cord and the baby's neck with no success. "I'm having a difficult

15

time getting it off."

"What does that mean?"

"Shh!" Shiphrah focused on adjusting the thick cord that had wound its way around the baby's delicate neck. "I can't get it. I'm going to have to cut it off." She grunted. "Puah, let Ziva take over your spot and come help me."

The younger women rushed to exchange positions.

"Here, grab the head and brace the shoulders." She adjusted her position to make room for the extra body between the woman's legs. Then she grabbed a sharp knife from beside her. "Give me a little more room."

Puah moved her fingers out of the way while delicately bearing the weight of the upper portion of the half-delivered baby.

Shiphrah slid the tip of her knife under the cord and pulled upwards away from the neck. A few more cuts and the cord fell away. "Big push for me."

Anta obliged with a deep thrust.

"Hold on," she instructed her apprentice.

"She's out!" Puah shouted as she fell back into a seated position with the baby in her arms.

Anta collapsed into the other two women and released her air.

"She's not breathing!" Puah's voice hit a high-pitched shrill as she screamed to her mentor, "She's not breathing!"

"I know," Shiphrah said. "Flip her over." She snatched a clean towel and vigorously rubbed the baby's back. "Come on!"

"What's happening?" Anta lifted herself to see.

"The cord cut off her air." She rubbed harder. "I'm trying to get her to breathe."

"My baby!" The mother covered her mouth as she wailed.

"Flip her over," the mentor demanded.

Puah carefully, but quickly adjusted the petite baby in her hands.

The older midwife placed her mouth over the newborn's nose and mouth and blew a few short breaths. "Come on, little one."

"Come on," Rania whispered.

Shiphrah snatched the baby from Puah's hands and placed her upside down in her own lap. She pounded on her back with the palm of her hand. "Breathe!" she commanded. "Please, breathe."

Puah rocked back and forth. "God of the universe," she prayed. "Hear the cry of your faithful midwives. Breathe life into this child."

Anta let out a monstrous howl and dropped onto Ziva's chest.

"Please, Lord. Return back the life of this little one." Shiphrah flipped the baby over and gave a few short breaths into her nose again. She bent over and placed her ear over the baby's face.

Everyone held their breath.

Shiphrah tucked her chin to her chest and

shook her head slightly before lifting her head to kiss the baby's forehead. "I'm sorry," she whispered.

"No!" Anta yelled. "You bring my baby back."

"There's nothing else I can do. The cord was wrapped too tight and possibly too long...I'm sorry."

"Leave me," she wept.

"I can help-"

"Leave!"

"Of course," Shiphrah said. She carefully wrapped the baby in a fresh cloth and handed the bundle to Ziva. "If she has any pain or-"

"I said leave!" Anta barked.

"As you wish."

The three midwives walked quietly out of the house and headed north. It wasn't until they reached the home they shared in Avaris before any of them spoke.

"I'll never get over that," Puah said, sorrow filling each word.

"No, you never do," Shiphrah said. "Never."

Chapter 2

"And the king of Egypt called for the midwives,"
-EXODUS 1:18

Carefully removing a few pieces of dried fish from a plate, Puah placed some into each of the bowls of lentils she had prepared. She and the other midwives worked so much away from the house that it was hard to keep meals ready. They tried to have one of the three of them stay to prepare food, but someone was always calling for their assistance.

Rania was out checking on patients. Shiphrah had just returned from a delivery. This morning had been Puah's turn to prepare food and she knew exactly what she wanted to eat.

One of their neighbors had brought them a large plate of fish a few days ago as a blessing. She had much success recently learning to fish from her husband and wanted to share the benefit beyond their small family. Puah had taken her mentor's advice and dried some for the coming days.

A smile warmed her face at the sight of a welcoming bowl of nourishment. She always imagined food as a way to embrace someone. Some days one just needed a good meal and a quiet moment to rest.

She reached over and grabbed a loaf of yeast bread. Tearing a few small fragments, she set them inside the bowls for dipping.

When a knock came at the door, her heart sank. She wiped her hands on a rag and waited a moment to see if Shiphrah moved to answer it. Silence urged her unwillingly into the courtyard.

With each step, she hesitated. Her skin felt as if it was tingling in the cold water of the Nile. Visitors were frequent, though much less so at this time of the day. Many would come calling for a birth or to seek medical advice. A knock at their door shouldn't have encouraged such trepidation, yet even the air around her felt different.

By the time she reached for the gate latch, her heart was pounding so loud it sounded like an impatient visitor knocking again.

She pulled open the door.

On the other side stood an ornately dressed Egyptian guard. His broad copper-toned chest shone bright in the sun. The top of her head barely reached the bottom of his ribs. Bright colors on his neck collar easily gave away his position within the royal guard.

"M-M-May I help you?" Puah managed to

stammer out the question.

"I am here seeking Shiphrah," the guard replied, without meeting the younger woman's eyes. His deep voice resonated through her and felt like it would shake her insides loose.

"I am she," Shiphrah said, appearing behind her.

Puah moved to the side so the older woman could speak with the official. She pressed her back against the stone wall for support.

"Your presence is required before Pharaoh Thutmose."

"When?"

"Now," he thundered.

"We'll go at once," she said and closed the gate.

"Why did you close the door on him?" Puah whispered. "Do you know who that is?"

"I know who he represents." Shiphrah took a deep breath. "Go get a bag ready. I need to pray."

"Pray?" She followed her mentor into one of the rooms. "Do we have time to be praying when there is a royal guard out there ready to take us to Pharaoh?"

"He can wait while we prepare." Shiphrah found a spot to kneel. "Do as I ask."

"As you wish." She left to obey. From the next room, Puah could hear her mentor praying aloud.

"God of the universe," Shiphrah called out with her head bowed to the ground. "Creator of all things. I don't know why Pharaoh seeks my presence, but everything inside me is stirred. Give me strength as I stand before him. Let me be respectful and humble. Give me boldness to speak when questioned and let all that I do bring honor to You."

Hear her cries to You, Lord, Puah prayed inwardly as her hands grabbed anything in sight to fill the bag. *Give my feet strength to stand beside her. Give my lips strength to remain closed.*

She stuffed a few more items into the bag and slung it over her shoulder. As she turned, her glance caught sight of the bowls she had left in the kitchen. With a deep sigh, she walked toward them. She carefully laid a clean towel over the food.

Her stomach growled, causing her to rub her midsection. She shook her head and stood in the doorway where her mentor knelt.

"Ready?" she called. The large shoulder bag hung by her side and a crooked smile lit up her face. "To meet a god?"

Shiphrah rose and wiped the dust from her dress. She took the bag off her apprentice's shoulder to move it to her own. "Very funny." She peered into the bag to double check its contents. "I only recognize one God and He doesn't wear a headdress." Closing the bag, she looked up. "At least I don't think He does."

Puah stifled a snort. "Let's go before that

guard breaks in here and drags us before Pharaoh."

It wasn't long before the two midwives had been guided through the streets of Peru-nefer and into Pharaoh's palace. The guard leading them had not wavered a single step to check on the two until they reached the entrance to the throne room. It was there that he stopped, turned to them, and pointed forward.

"The midwives you summoned," an aide announced as they approached.

"Ahh, yes." Pharaoh nodded. His gold and blue striped headdress bounced with the movement. "Step forward."

They obeyed.

Puah knelt as low to the ground as she could manage just as Shiphrah had instructed her. The coolness of the tile, felt through her worn dress, sent a shiver coursing to the top of her head and back down to her toes.

"Rise," Pharaoh Thutmose voiced.

Puah rose to her feet to look at the god on earth the Egyptians feared above all else.

He sat as straight as an iron rod upon a raised golden throne. His broad chest matched those of his guards, though his was somewhat wrinkled with age. Aides and guards surrounded him waiting for their next assignments.

"I have called you here today to hand down an order. Shiphrah." He paused.

The older woman took a small step forward.

"Your name has been spread throughout my land as the best midwife upon whom one can call. I have also heard that you see fit to teach others your trade." He set his gaze on Puah.

She swallowed the large lump in her throat and turned her sights to the decorations on the floor. The tiles were hand-painted with varying symbols. They told a story, but she was too frightened to try to decipher it.

"It's as you have said, mighty Pharaoh." Shiphrah's Egyptian words were smooth in Puah's ear. It did much to calm her rapid heartbeat.

"Then my information is correct. Good," his voice was as steady as a rushing stream and carried just as strongly through the large room. "So, seeing as you seem to instruct the others of your craft as an authority, I need you to pass along the following edict. When you are performing your duties as a midwife to the Hebrew women and see them upon the birthing stones, if you see her give birth to a son, then you shall kill him. If the child is a daughter, then she shall live."

Puah fought back a whimper. Her stomach rumbled and bubbled, causing her to feel light headed. A vision of the uneaten bowl of lentils and bread sung out to her. She tried to focus on the bright colors under her feet as her breathing became short and strenuous. She feared passing out.

"This is your edict?" Shiphrah asked without meeting his eyes.

"Yes."

"I understand."

"Then you are dismissed." Pharaoh waved them away.

Puah caught Shiphrah's form bending in half and backing slowly away beside her. She bowed and stepped a wobbly foot backward, but stumbled. The move forced her to set a knee down to steady herself. She shuddered and held her breath.

Daring a peek under her fallen strands of hair, she realized the others in the room didn't notice her at all. She attempted to back away again with success this time.

Out of the throne room, she searched in every direction for her mentor. The long hallways and varied paths intimidated her steps. When she caught sight of brisk movement, she hurried to Shiphrah's side.

"We are not seriously going to kill Hebrew boys, are we?" she asked in a whispered, but severe Hebrew tongue as she effortlessly caught up with the older woman.

The mentor continued her pace without a response.

"Shiphrah," Puah stepped in front to stop her. "Tell me we're not going to kill innocent children. Please tell me we will not."

She folded her arms across her chest before shaking her head. "No, we're not."

"Good," Puah said with a stomp.

"Shh." Shiphrah put her finger to her lips. "The guards don't understand you, but the royals study many languages. If one of them should happen to hear you, we could both lose our necks."

She pulled Puah aside into an empty room and glanced around before speaking, "This came directly from Pharaoh. I'll have to come up with a plan to get around this edict. Give me time to think and then I'll need you to follow my instructions."

"Of course."

"It won't be easy and we'll need to enlist the aid of every midwife in the guild willing to accept the risk."

"There isn't one I can think of who wouldn't."

Shiphrah stretched her neck to move her face closer to Puah's. "This is not a light matter, my young learner. Disobedience could mean certain death."

She squared her pointy shoulders. "Murder is strictly forbidden by God. I'd rather deal with man's wrath than God's."

"I hope everyone sees it that way." She looked around once more and slowly stepped back into the corridor. "Remember, they believe Pharaoh to be a powerful god. It'll be hard to persuade our Egyptian students of a bigger One."

"Then we will seek His help in convincing them."

"Hello," a melodious voice called in Egyptian from the end of one of the hallways.

Shiphrah squinted her aging eyes in order to sharpen her vision. "My princess," she said with a bow and switched her tongue easily from Hebrew to Egyptian to greet her.

A slender built girl of fifteen with an attractive oval face practically floated in their direction. Her almond-shaped eyes shone bright with youth and vigor. Her delicate pointed chin was held high with her position as she approached them.

"I'd like to introduce one of my apprentices. This is Puah."

"Greetings, Princess Hatshepsut," Puah said in faltering Egyptian. She had been practicing under the teaching of Shiphrah but hadn't yet been required to speak in front of a royal. "It is a pleasure to meet you."

"Have you come to spend time with me today?" She folded her hands in front of her like a small child.

"I'm afraid not," Shiphrah answered. "We've just come from being called to see your father and have much business to attend to."

"That is everyone's excuse." She rolled her large eyes. Their color reminded Puah of polished hematite.

"With sincere apologies, I'm afraid it's quite

true for us."

"Very well." She sighed. "I shall accept it this time." A raised eyebrow let the two women know she meant no harm in her words.

"You are a most gracious princess." Shiphrah bowed.

"Away with you then before I change my mind," she teased.

"We shall return another day," the older woman promised. "When we are not so pressed with duty."

"It was an honor." Puah bowed.

Princess Hatshepsut waved them off and went in search of another form of entertainment.

"Do you suppose she heard us talking?" the young student asked in Hebrew when they had cleared the palace's main gate.

"I don't believe so. She is still young and probably doesn't know much Hebrew yet."

She breathed a sigh of relief.

"At least she didn't lead on that she heard any of our planning. Though headstrong, she is pretty harmless. Her main concerns are often of enjoying life. She has not been privy to much royal business as of yet."

"She acted like we were there to play with her."

"I wouldn't put it past her." Shiphrah grinned. "In our culture, she would already be married or someone's apprentice by now. In her position, nothing much is required of her except to study and stay out of the way. I'm sure that kind of life dulls her, so she seeks out excitement."

"Of which you've provided previously?"

"My mentor had ties to the palace." She shrugged. "I've frequently visited, though before today I have never had to stand before Pharaoh in any sort of official summons. There were several occasions we spent the day as entertainment."

She scrunched her nose. "Like their pet monkeys?"

"Don't judge." Her mentor bumped against her. "Sometimes, one must do things they wouldn't choose in order to keep good relations."

Puah prayed silently as they continued their walk back home. She knew her mentor was doing the same in the quiet that stayed between them on their trip.

When they entered the courtyard, Rania was waiting for them.

"How did the checkup go?" Shiphrah asked.

"She's doing well. Where did you two journey off to?"

"The palace," Puah answered.

Rania dropped the cloth from her hand. "What?"

"We were summoned before Pharaoh," Shiphrah explained.

"What did he want?" She stepped closer to the two of them.

"To kill innocent children." Puah huffed and

crossed her arms.

"I don't understand."

"An edict." The mentor returned her bag to its easily accessible place. "To kill all Hebrew male children as soon as they are born."

"Why would he order such a thing?"

"Because he's scared," Puah said as she tightened the grip of her arms.

"Of children?"

"Of our people," Shiphrah clarified.

"And this is his solution?"

"For now." She paced around the open courtyard.

"We can't kill children." Rania shrugged. "Can we?"

"Of course not," Puah defended. "That goes against our calling. It goes against our belief. It goes a-a-against life!"

"But if Pharaoh has ordered it…"

"Then we shall do it," Shiphrah said without missing a step.

The two younger women exchanged a horrified glance.

"At least we'll make him think we are," Shiphrah went on. "Gather the guild. I'll share my plan with everyone at once."

Puah glanced into the kitchen. Making her way toward the two bowls that still sat under the towel where she had left them, she reached for hers. Something that had seemed the most important thing in the moment now paled in comparison with what lay ahead. As hungry as she was for food to nourish her body, she knew spreading Shiphrah's call was of much more importance.

"Here." She handed the bowl to Rania. "I'll head west."

Messengers were sent far and wide to all corners of Egypt for the midwives to come. They gathered together in the large valley between Goshen and the south lands.

"Ladies," the mentor called above the crowd. "I have an important message from Pharaoh."

"Pharaoh?" whispers flew through the crowd as they quieted.

"Pharaoh Thutmose has declared an edict. As we perform our duties as midwives to Hebrew women, we are to kill any child that is born a boy. The girls are to remain alive."

"Murder!"

"Sin!"

"Outrage!"

Shouts roared.

"Ladies, please!" Shiphrah raised her hands for their attention. "I don't plan on obeying this order myself, but I'm required to pass along the message."

"What will we do?"

"Disobedience means death!"

"Here's what we are going to do!" She shouted

for their attention and focus. "We'll continue as normal. We will spread Pharaoh's edict because he will be checking on that, but we will also pass along more. We'll instruct all midwives to take their time going to help at a Hebrew birth. We will wait until we are called by the women who are with them and then we'll slowly make our way to their homes."

"Do you think that will work?" Rania asked beside her.

"I'm not sure." Shiphrah paused. "At least the babies will be born. I simply pray we won't be late to assist if anything should go wrong. It will be easy to spread the news quickly and also leave a few supplies at the homes of those who will be giving birth soon, so they will have what they need when the time comes."

She turned back to the gathering. "Now go. Go throughout the land and spread this message. Only keep our true intent within the guild."

"I think it went well," Puah said as the crowd thinned. "What's our next step?"

"Let me think." Shiphrah pinched her forehead between her thumb and first finger. "Most of the Hebrew women who are heavily pregnant have delivered before, so that shouldn't be a problem." She became quiet as she ran through the list of names in her mind. "Jochebed, she's pregnant again. She'll be a great asset to us. She can help spread the word to the women in

Goshen about what is happening. We need to go see her."

"What about Egyptian women?" Rania asked.

"Pharaoh's edict was only for Hebrews."

"What I mean is do you think they could help?"

Shiphrah thought for a long moment. "We'll keep it simply to our guild and the Hebrews for now. If it comes to that, we'll approach the matter carefully."

"I'm sure many would be willing to help."

"I'm sure many would." The mentor smiled a weary smile. "I simply want to remain cautious and spare as many necks as possible. If we don't have to endanger them, then we won't."

"I understand. I'll grab a bag," Rania offered.

"I'll go pray," Puah said.

By the end of the day, the three midwives sat in the home of Jochebed.

"I was certainly surprised by your visit," the woman said. "Though I never turn away guests."

Jochebed sat reclined on a small pillow. Her face held peace and her body relaxed. She was a well-known woman in their land for her hospitality and grace. She was seen as a second mother to many young women and a friend to many others. No one was ever turned away at her gate.

"I wish this was a social call or even a matter of checking in on your health."

"Oh?" Jochebed straightened.

"Yes. You see Pharaoh has…how do I say this…"

"Ordered us to kill babies," Puah irrupted.

"What!" Jochebed gasped.

"It's true," Rania agreed.

"Hold your tongues and let me speak," the mentor scolded.

The younger women leaned back and tightened their lips.

Shiphrah faced Jochebed. "It's true. Pharaoh has decreed that we kill any Hebrew boy born from henceforth. We are allowed to let the girls live, but we must kill all boys."

"That's monstrous." She held her round belly. "He can't do such a thing."

"He can and he has," Shiphrah stated simply. "But we've got a plan. We'll need your help."

"Anything."

"We need to spread the word as quickly as possible. My guild is spreading the word through the south lands. I need your help in telling all Hebrew women here in Goshen about the edict, but also inform them of our plan. Tell them not to call until after they've delivered."

"What if they need a midwife before then?"

"If they have to call earlier, then one will arrive anyway. We shall handle each problem as it comes, but our people are strong and we will be praying even more so for all the ones under our care."

"I will be praying too."

"Good. We'll need all the help God is willing to offer."

"What else can we do?"

"I'm going to encourage our people to share supplies as well. We need to take care of each other now more than ever."

"Of course." Jochebed reached her swollen fingers out and grabbed the hand of Shiphrah. "God will give you strength and wisdom."

"I don't take this on lightly. Disobeying Pharaoh's order could mean death for me and any others found assisting us."

"Our God is far greater than Pharaoh. He has never left our people and He never will."

"I wish every Hebrew had your faith." She squeezed back.

Chapter 3

"But the midwives feared God, and did not as the king of Egypt commanded them, but saved the men children alive."
-EXODUS 1:15

Shiphrah stepped out of a home in Avaris with a bag full of supplies. "Thank you." She waved to the family inside.

Puah had already walked into the street and was waiting for her. "And?"

She looked into the bag. "Fresh vegetables and some other things. We'll bring them to our next stop."

"Shiphrah," Rania called as she approached them at full speed. "A guard was just at the house looking for you. You've been summoned to appear before Pharaoh again."

"It's only been a few months, what do you think he wants?" Puah asked her mentor.

"I don't know, but we better appear as soon as possible."

Puah nodded.

"Rania." Shiphrah shoved the bag toward her. "Take this to Uma and do a check on her. Once you're done, go back to the house and be available in case someone comes calling for us."

"Are you sure you don't want me to accompany you?"

"Pharaoh has already seen Puah. I don't want your face to be added to his line of fire."

"Of course."

Shiphrah and Puah rushed south toward Peru-nefer. There they were granted entrance at the palace gates and ushered quickly to the throne room with bowed heads and hearts filled with silent prayers.

As soon as the two women were announced, Pharaoh questioned them, "Do you consider me a fool?"

"No," Shiphrah spoke for the two of them.

"Then why have you done this thing? Why have you disobeyed my order and kept the male children alive?" His chest heaved and grew red. "I receive reports every day of the increase of Hebrews."

"Mighty Pharaoh." Shiphrah kept her eyes to the exceedingly decorated floor in the hopes her voice would not reveal her fear. "The Hebrew women are not like the Egyptian women. They are strong and deliver their children before a midwife can arrive."

"Very well," he said and was silent for a few minutes. "If you cannot carry out my orders, then I will call on others to do so. Let my new edict go out to all people," his husky voice rose in timbre as if all Egypt could hear him from his throne. "All Hebrews are to throw their newborn sons into the Nile, but they can allow the girls to live. My guards will be stationed at points along the river to ensure this order is followed."

The two women bowed and left the palace.

"Now what are we going to do?" Puah asked once they had passed through the gates.

"Use the network. We'll hide as many babies as we can. Pharaoh's focus will be on Goshen. We'll move as many babies south as possible." She hurried her pace. "Let's also see if Rania can convince some of the Egyptian women to help us."

"And what of the guards? They'll certainly notice an absence of babies being thrown into the river."

"I've already got a plan for them as well."

Upon arriving at their home, Shiphrah got to work. She grabbed a fresh set of linens and brought them over to Puah. "Look." She laid one out on the table and pretended to wrap it like she would with a newborn. "We'll take the linens we use to clean the baby and wrap some meat in it. You and Rania can get the baby to a safe house while I help the mother take the bundle to the river. The guards will see us toss the bundle into the river and the crocodiles will devour the meat so no evidence remains."

"That's sharp thinking."

"We need to make sure we wrap the meat bundles in the bloody cloths so it will be devoured and the guards will see the blood as proof we have fulfilled the edict." She unwrapped the cloth and refolded it to return it to its original place.

"I guess I need to start collecting any meat families can spare."

"Not an easy task, I know." She turned to face Puah.

"Maybe some of the Egyptian women would be willing to offer meat along with help?"

"If you think we can ask without placing them in danger."

"We've all passed the point of danger when we began this course of disobedience."

"I don't want others to die for me."

"We aren't doing any of this for you," Puah assured her. "We're doing this because it's the right thing to do."

"Shiphrah." Rania rushed into the room. Her cheeks were flush. "Come quick!"

"What is it?"

"Jochebed."

Shiphrah loaded prepared bags of supplies and instruments across her body and headed out the door.

Puah and Rania followed closely behind.

When the three women reached Jochebed's home, they didn't stop to knock at the gate.

"I'm here," Shiphrah announced as she hurried through the courtyard and into the house.

"Thank God," Dinah, Jochebed's neighbor, said with clasped hands. "I stopped by to check on her and found her in pain."

"When?" Shiphrah asked.

"This morning. We tried delivering on our own just as you instructed."

"I'm here." She came to the bent over woman's side and wiped Jochebed's forehead.

The woman attempted a smile, but it fell flat. "He's coming, but it doesn't feel like the others."

"Ladies," Shiphrah called over her shoulder.

The two apprentices went to work preparing for the arrival of another Hebrew.

Puah was arranging a stack of linens when she felt someone watching her. She glanced over her shoulder to see a young girl standing in the doorway holding her younger brother on her hip. "Hello, Miriam."

The shy seven-year-old bowed her head. Her straight, long black hair created a veil over her face.

"Do you remember me?"

She nodded, causing her hair to flow back and forth with the movement. "You helped with my brother."

"That's right."

Jochebed's second child, Aaron, was Puah's first delivery three years ago. She wasn't far removed from being branded a child herself at the ripe age of twelve.

"He's gotten big."

Miriam rubbed her forehead against her brother's. Eyes as dark and rich as the soil by the Nile peered up at Puah through her hair and then moved to her mother. "Is momma hurt?"

"No, she is about to give you another sibling. We're here helping just like we did with Aaron." She pointed to the young boy.

"I hope it's a girl this time."

Puah smiled. "You don't like your brother?"

"I like him just fine." She adjusted the toddler on her small hip. "But I'd like a girl to play with too."

She laughed. "Why don't you take Aaron to go play while we help your mother. I'll come get you when the baby is here."

Miriam nodded and turned to leave.

Puah went back to her work, but a few moments later, she felt something tug her sleeve. She turned to see Miriam again. "I thought you went to play with your brother."

"He needed a nap anyway."

"Would you like to help me then?"

"Can I?" Her eyes grew large.

"Of course. We could always use more hands."

Miriam followed Puah's every instruction

while they worked together.

After they finished, the young girl stared at her mother. "She doesn't look happy."

Puah followed her gaze to see Shiphrah instructing Jochebed to adjust to a new position. "Sometimes, delivery can be hard."

"I've had dreams about him."

"Him? I thought you said you wanted a sister."

Miriam turned back toward Puah. "I did. That's what I've been praying for too."

"What's your dream about?"

"Him." She motioned over her shoulder to her mother with her pointed chin. "Momma has him, but then she puts him in the river." She was quiet for a long moment as large tears streamed down her smooth cheeks. "Do we have to feed him to the crocodiles?"

Puah looked over the girl's head to the group of women who encircled the expectant mother. "If I tell you something, can you protect the secret?"

Miriam met her eyes and nodded.

"We're not going to put him in the river." She wiped the girls' wet face with a cloth.

"But everyone said…"

"I know," she whispered. "But God has told us it's not right to kill."

"But in my dream…"

"We have a plan." She smiled, hoping to ease the young girl's fears.

Hours later, Puah held tight to Jochebed's

arm. Beginning the final stages of labor, the mentor had them move her to the birthing stones. Puah and Rania had taken their usual place on either side of the expectant mother. Shiphrah knelt under them to deliver the baby.

"Breathe," Puah reminded Jochebed.

Jochebed bore down.

"He's here," Shiphrah said below them.

She helped Jochebed ease off the birthing stones and onto something softer.

"Here you are." Shiphrah handed Jochebed her freshly wrapped newborn.

"Hello, little one," Jochebed said as she kissed his forehead. "Shh, there, there, my son."

The baby quieted down as he snuggled into his mother's chest.

"She'll take over for a few moments while I get her cleaned up," Shiphrah instructed. "She already knows what to do."

Puah and Rania helped prepare a mixture and spread it on a cloth.

Shiphrah gently, but thoroughly cleaned Jochebed and applied the healing pack.

"There, that will do for now," she said as she moved her attention back to the baby. "Is he finished?"

Jochebed nodded and then yawned.

"Rest now," Shiphrah said as she retrieved the baby boy. "You need to gather your strength. We still have another step in the plan."

Jochebed smiled contently at her son before letting her take him. "I think I will take a rest now, but please don't take him yet. I want a few more minutes with him before we go."

"Just a few."

Puah fetched Miriam and Aaron and brought them to Jochebed's side. "See," she whispered in Miriam's ear. "She's just fine."

Shiphrah handed the boy to Rania.

"He's gorgeous," the woman commented. "I've never seen a more handsome child."

"Is everything prepared?"

"Yes." She nuzzled the boy. "I've sent word to the family. They are expecting him. It's getting close to sunset. We'll need to leave as soon as night covers the streets."

"Agreed." The mentor gathered the bloody cloth she had used to clean the boy and wrapped a small bundle of meat inside. She took it over to Jochebed and handed it to her. "Ready?"

She nodded. "I'll go with you to the river, but they are not taking my baby anywhere."

"What are you talking about?"

"I'll trick the guards, but my baby is staying here with me."

"We've discussed this."

"I know."

"Then you understand we've made arrangements to hide him?" She motioned to Rania, who held the bundle tightly to her chest.

"I know that too, but he'll be safer with me."

"I can assure you he'd be better off if he's taken away to another place."

"Your plan will purchase us time. Maybe by then, Pharaoh will move on to another way to oppress our people and leave my son alone."

"I doubt such."

"Please," she folded her fingers. "I know I can hide him here."

"I can't force you to do anything." She huffed. "Let's get down to the river before it's too late."

The two women took the wrapped meat and made their way to the Nile.

Just as expected, a pair of guards stood nearby.

"Weep," Shiphrah whispered.

Jochebed let out a wail. "Oh, my baby!"

She snatched the bundle out of her arms and rushed toward the water. "You heard Pharaoh. Into the river he goes!" She waded in as deep as she dared before tossing the bundle as far as she could.

"My baby!" The mother dropped to her knees in the muddy banks and reached for the water.

Flashes of dark green and blue mixed where the bundle had landed.

Shiphrah silently thanked God that the crocodiles were hungry enough to accept the package and not give chase to her. They were more temperamental than Pharaoh.

She swam back as fast as her legs would kick.

She trudged through the muddy banks to where the previously pregnant woman crawled. The lower half of her dress now soaking wet made moving all the more difficult.

Helping Jochebed rise to her feet, she let the woman lean on her.

Another mother and midwife came dragging to the edge of the river.

The mentor exchanged glances with the midwife. She had been one of her former apprentices and the woman she huddled next to was a friend. Each gave a subtle nod as they passed. The young mother wept and cradled the bundle tighter to her chest.

Shiphrah could see blood from the cloth run between her fingers.

Another feast for the crocodiles.

The older woman shot the guards a dirty look as they ignored her.

"Excellent work," Shiphrah complemented her patient when they were far enough away.

"Let's just hope it was enough to keep them away for a while." She wiped her face with her wet sleeves.

Clustered together, the women sauntered back toward Jochebed's home.

"Has she lost her senses?" Puah asked upon their return after Shiphrah had filled her in on the mother's plan.

"Just what I said," Jochebed interjected. "I'm

going to hide him myself."

"Listen to reason," Shiphrah urged. "He's not safe here. We've found homes to move the males. Places where they are well looked after."

"He needs to be here with me."

"They'll eventually come for him," Rania added. "He's a newborn who needs constant care. How will you hide him?"

"I've been working a few places in the wall to secure him." She took them to one of the places and moved part of the stone away. "See?"

"And what if he cries?" Shiphrah asked. "Your other children are old enough now that you won't be able to use them as an excuse."

Jochebed closed her eyes and turned away.

"And what of Mariam?"

She spun around to face Shiphrah. "What?"

"Do you expect a child so young to lie to Egyptian guards?"

"She's a smart girl."

"You're willing to place her in that position?"

Jochebed took her baby from Rania and cradled him to her chest. She sang a soft lullaby in his ear.

Shiphrah sighed. "I know this is difficult."

"What do you know? You've never been asked to give up a child before."

The older woman looked between her sandaled feet.

Jochebed softened. "Oh, I'm sorry. I shouldn't

have said-"

She held up her hand. "I know how difficult this must be for you. What I'm asking is hard, but necessary. If we don't hide him, he'll die. Your neck will be in danger as well."

"I appreciate all that you are doing for our people. I do. I'm happy to help in whatever way I can, but I'm not giving up my son." She rocked the baby in her arms.

"If you insist. Just know I can't protect him if you keep him here."

"I understand."

Shiphrah gazed at the small boy. "I can't get over how handsome he is."

"I know." She beamed at the boy.

"Have you chosen a name yet?" Puah asked.

"None seems fitting enough for him."

"We must be going now," Rania offered. She placed one of the bags across her body. "No sense attracting any more attention than necessary."

"I have some food to share with the others." She pointed toward the kitchen.

"I'll be happy to accept the gift," the mentor said and made her way into the kitchen.

The two young midwives in training finished collecting the supplies they had brought with them.

Rania stood waiting in the open courtyard.

Puah went to Jochebed's side. "He certainly is very handsome."

The mother hummed.

She bent down to kiss the boy's forehead. "May God bless you, precious child. May He keep you safe and give you the chance to grow old with your people." She looked up into Jochebed's watery eyes. "You're sure you won't reconsider? It's not too late."

"No." She shook her head. "He belongs here with his family."

"Shame. The family in Thebes will surely be disappointed not to be able to welcome this little bundle into their arms."

"Are we ready, ladies?" Shiphrah emerged from the kitchen with two packs of supplies.

Puah nodded and kissed the baby one last time.

The mentor passed the mother without a glance over her shoulder.

"One more thing." Jochebed reached for Shiphrah's sleeve.

"Yes?"

"I'd like to pray for you." She turned toward the courtyard. "All of you."

Rania dropped the bag at the gate and walked toward them.

"That I'll also accept," the mentor agreed.

The women huddled together on their knees in the small room.

Jochebed sat in the middle of the group with her newborn in her arms. Each midwife placed a hand on her as she prayed.

"God of the universe." She rocked her baby. "We humbly ask You to keep Your protective hand over these midwives and the others. They are stepping out in faith that You are bigger than Pharaoh. Give them strength to keep trusting You. Give them wisdom and an extra sense to know when danger is coming. Help them as they seek to do Your work. Bless the mothers who are pregnant even now as they prepare to deliver their children into the world. We pray that You will one day deliver us. Make Your face to shine upon them and may they be blessed for their faithfulness to You."

Chapter 4

*"And when she could no longer hide him, she
took for him an ark of bulrushes,"*
-EXODUS 2:3

Eight days after Jochebed's baby was born, the
midwives were requested at her home.

"Is she unwell?" Shiphrah asked as the three
midwives walked along the quiet streets.

"She didn't seem to be," Rania answered as she
led the group. "She simply sent word that we all
come tonight."

"Do you think she's finally come to her
senses?" Puah asked as she tucked a few loose
strands of hair back under her headcloth and
adjusted the bag on her shoulder.

"I sure hope so," the older woman said. "I
really do."

"Greetings." Jochebed beamed at the women
as they approached her home. She was standing
just outside the gate waiting for their arrival. "I'm
so glad you could come."

"Thank you," Shiphrah said, entering the gate into the open courtyard. "I wish I knew why you called us."

"You know my husband, Amram." The woman waved to the man standing inside.

He was tall and stood with his hands folded in front of him. His simple tunic hung loose and his face gave no indication of the type of request that was about to be asked. Puah thought he looked much like an Egyptian guard. No emotion showed either way.

"Greetings," her mentor said with a bow. "It's a pleasure to see you again."

Puah and Rania each bowed their head toward him in turn.

He stepped closer to them. "My wife tells me you assisted with her birth."

"She speaks truth."

"She also tells me you are very knowledgeable in medicine and the body." He rubbed his thick beard.

"I do what I can to help our people."

"Miriam," he called without looking away from them.

The young girl entered the room with a bundle in her arms.

"Yes, Father?"

"We're ready now."

Miriam brought the wrapped cloth to her father and stepped to her mother's side.

"Would you be humble enough to help us sanctify our son to the Lord?" He stretched the wrapped baby toward them "We couldn't risk letting others know he was still here."

"It would be a great honor."

"Miriam, clear that table there."

"Yes, Father." The girl hurried to obey.

Jochebed moved to place meager supplies on the table without waiting to be instructed.

"That'll do fine," Shiphrah said.

Amram placed the baby on the prepared area.

Puah and Rania moved to stand near the table with their mentor and the parents.

Amram unwrapped the cloth from around the boy and placed his hands upon him. Words of prayer flowed over his tongue as the women listened. He moved to pick up a knife without pause.

"What's he doing?" Rania whispered to Puah.

"It's part of our custom."

"What's he going to do with that knife?"

"Shh, just watch." She placed a finger to her lips and then pointed toward the baby. "He will not harm the child."

Jochebed placed her hands on the baby's shoulders.

"Puah…" Rania said, drawing out her name.

"Be still," she said sternly and squeezed her Egyptian counterpart's arm for reinforcement.

Amram's prayer continued as he reached for

the boy's delicate part and coaxed its foreskin up. His other hand lined the knife against the connected place.

"He's not!" the midwife in training muffled a scream of disapproval.

"It is not your place to interfere," Puah said, pulling her arm. "Peace."

With a skilled slice, Amram cut the foreskin clean off.

The baby let out a loud wail.

Like lightning, Shiphrah immediately covered the bleeding area and applied pressure until it stopped.

"I think I'm going to be sick." Rania stepped out into the open courtyard with her hands over her mouth.

Puah followed her. "He's unharmed."

"That man just cut off the boy's-"

"Just a small portion of it. This is part of our custom."

"I've heard you Hebrews are strange, but this?" She expanded a hand toward the room for emphasis.

Puah wound her fingers around Rania's wrist and pulled. "Come." She led her back to where Shiphrah stood with Jochebed. "See for yourself."

Rania peered over the woman's arms into the sleeping face of the baby.

"See," she said. "He is well."

"He seems unharmed." Rania's shoulders

lowered. "All of your males have this done to them?"

"It's how we distinguish ourselves from other people. It's a covenant handed down from our God to our ancestor Abraham as a sign of distinction and separation."

"Well, I could sure think of other ways you could do that." Rania brushed the baby's cheek with her finger.

"We were not the ones who chose it," Jochebed said.

"Can you imagine any male choosing to let that be done to himself?" Shiphrah asked.

"No," Rania said thoughtfully. "I suppose they wouldn't. But they do choose to obey God to do it to their sons."

"Just as you would obey something your Egyptian gods ordered you to do."

"Yes," Rania said, letting the anger melt from her voice. "I guess I would."

Three months later, Puah and Shiphrah visited Jochebed in her home on their rounds through Avaris.

"You did what with the boy?" the older midwife shouted.

"Put him in the Nile," Jochebed stated with no

emotion.

"The one place we were trying to keep him out of!" She threw her hands in the air. "I wish you would have listened to me. He could have been safe in one of our hiding houses."

"I know, but you don't understand," the mother pleaded. "I didn't just toss him in the river as crocodile food."

Shiphrah sucked in a breath and held it waiting for an explanation.

"I made a basket with the strongest bulrushes I could find. I wove them tight and pitched the outside so water would not leak inside."

"Like a boat?" Puah asked.

"Yes, like a boat. I put him in among the reeds. I found a spot where the current is not very strong."

"Why?" the mentor begged.

"I couldn't hide him anymore. He was getting too big."

"I told you I could hide him."

"I-"

"Mother!" Miriam rushed into the courtyard. "Come quickly!"

"What is it, Daughter?"

"The baby."

Jochebed hurried toward her. "What has happened?"

"After you put him in the river, I stayed back to watch what would happen." She lowered her head a bit. "Forgive me."

"What did you see?"

"The princess, Momma. She was washing in the Nile and saw your little ark. She had one of her maidens fetch it and they discovered the baby."

Puah's heart raced. "What did she do with him?"

"She took him back to the palace. She said she was going to keep him."

"How do you know all of this?" Shiphrah asked.

"When I saw the maiden take the basket out from the reeds, I followed her and told the princess that I would fetch her a milk nurse for the baby."

"Jochebed." Shiphrah turned to her. "Go quickly to offer yourself."

Puah followed Shiphrah, Jochebed, and Miriam toward the palace.

"Here is a Hebrew to nurse the baby," Miriam said to the princess' maid when they entered the gates.

"You've done well, child," she answered. The woman stood proud and proper. Her beautifully wrapped dress fit her body perfectly. A bright smile warmed her face. "Come with me."

The maiden guided them deep into the palace complex to the princess' chamber.

Soft white linens which hung from the ceiling waved in the breeze coming from the open porch.

Each piece of furniture was meticulously placed. Statues and paintings of lionesses, the princess' favorite animal, covered much of the area.

"Shiphrah, it is good to see you again." Princess Hatshepsut stood in the archway leading to the porch. She was still a young girl, but her stance somehow was one of a grown woman. She stood taller. Prouder.

She bowed. "And you, Princess."

"What a happy fortune you have come." The royal woman stepped lightly toward them.

"Oh?"

"Why yes." She extended the bundle in her arms. "Look what I have pulled from the Nile."

"He's a Hebrew."

"I thought so." She pulled him in close and ran her finger softly down the top of his nose. "He is very handsome."

"Indeed."

"My lady," the maid said. "We've found a milk nurse for him." She waved to Jochebed. She wore a dress that had been hemmed so many times it looked like a collection of other dresses. Her face was dirty from working to prepare food all morning.

The mother bowed deeply. "I'm at the humble assistance of my princess."

"You have experience I trust."

"Yes, my lady." She bowed again. "I've nursed my own strong children. All of whom are healthy."

"Very well. You shall take the boy, nurse him until he is weaned, and I shall give you wages."

"As you request."

"But first," she said. "Shiphrah, would you mind looking him over for me?"

"It would be my pleasure." She took the boy to the massive bed and gave him a full examination. Upon returning him to the princess's waiting arms, she reported, "He's strong and healthy."

"He will make an excellent addition to our family." Princess Hatshepsut laughed as the baby cooed. "One last thing. What to call you?" She hummed to herself as she swayed. "I know. I'll call you Moses since you are a child I drew out of the water."

"An excellent name," Shiphrah agreed. "I'm sure your father will be very proud of the variation of his name."

"I think so too." She beamed.

"My lady?" the maid asked.

"Yes?"

She motioned to Jochebed with her eyes.

"Oh, yes." The princess walked to the Hebrew woman and delicately placed the baby in her arms. "Now, spare nothing on him. If you need more wages than I send with you, let my guards know. I will be sure that he has everything he needs to grow strong."

"It will be as you have said." Jochebed huddled the boy to her chest.

"Until we are united once again, dear Moses." She kissed her fingertip and placed it on his forehead. "May Ra fly with you and be your guide."

Once the midwives and mother had returned to Jochebed's home, they all marveled at the young boy who had not only been pulled from the Nile but returned to his mother's arms. In addition, the Princess of Egypt was going to pay Jochebed to raise her own child. Each stood in utter amazement at the day's events.

"Only God," Puah assessed staring down at the sleeping child in his mother's arms.

The others nodded in unison.

"With the short time I have with you, Moses," Jochebed spoke softly. "I'm going to tell you all about our God." She rocked the boy as she paced around the open courtyard.

A cool breeze blew in to refresh the sticky heat that was quickly turning into night. Puah closed her eyes and soaked in its calming effect. The day had been a whirlwind of emotion and activity. It was nice to sit and take a break. The cool clay bowl in her hands filled with boiled vegetables promised nourishment to her stomach. The collection of friends invited nourishment for her soul.

Jochebed eased her voice into the familiar story handed down from generation to generation. "In the beginning…"

Chapter 5

"And the child grew, and she brought him unto Pharaoh's daughter, and he became her son."
-EXODUS 2:10

1514 B.C.

The three midwives rushed through the palace hallways and down a long corridor.

"This way," Queen Hatshepsut's maiden urged them on.

After her father's recent death, her husband, Thutmose II, had taken over the throne, making Hatshepsut Queen of Egypt.

"When did the pains begin?" Shiphrah asked, fighting to keep air in her aged lungs.

"Last night," the maiden called over her shoulder. "I asked if I could fetch you then, but she thought it wasn't time yet."

"Being stubborn is more like it," Puah added restraining her speed to keep her mentor in sight.

"She always has been."

The women entered the chamber shortly after

the maiden.

A woman's scream directed them to a couch where the Queen lay.

"We're here!" Puah shouted as she rushed toward the sound.

"Thank Ra." Queen Hatshepsut grunted.

Shiphrah made it to her side and took a few deep breaths. "Tell me what's going on."

"Pains," she answered, rubbing her mid-section. "All over and a tightness that has been happening all night."

"Fresh linens," Shiphrah instructed the maid. "And get clean water mixed with wine."

"I'll check her," Puah offered. "Take a minute to catch your breath."

Shiphrah nodded and sat on a nearby stool.

"My lady, please come with me to the bed." She held out her arm. "I need to check you."

Queen Hatshepsut rose slightly, but couldn't straighten all the way. "It hurts so much."

"We'll take it slow." She slid her arm under the woman's elbow to help bear her weight.

"Close," Puah reported after examining her. "She's definitely in labor."

"Why didn't you send for me when this started?" Shiphrah asked, finally being able to steady her breaths.

"I wanted to be strong like your Hebrew women."

"There is no weakness in calling for help when

it's needed. You are too much like the young princess who always insisted on her way. You are Queen of all Egypt now."

"And so, I must be strong for my people." She groaned and rubbed her stomach.

"And so, you must learn to take care of yourself."

"Ahh!" She roared much like the lionesses she favored.

"Let's get you set up." Shiphrah rose and joined them. "We can set up the birthing stones right over there." She pointed to an open area in the middle of the room.

"Birthing stones?" the maid asked with a gasp.

"The best way to give birth."

The maid looked to the queen and back at the midwife.

She cleared her throat. "In my opinion, that is."

"I trust you," Queen Hatshepsut offered.

A few short hours later, the queen started her final pushes.

"Keep bearing down," the mentor instructed.

The royal woman's face turned from copper-toned to a deep crimson.

Puah held on to her arm and prayed they both could keep up their strength.

"She's here!" the older woman announced.

"A...girl..." the queen panted. Her body hung between the two apprentices like a dead animal.

"Yes."

"Why isn't she crying?" Puah asked.

"Probably just some fluid in her lungs." She turned the baby over in her hands and tilted her slightly down.

With a few quick pats, the baby coughed up a small amount of liquid. Then she let out a loud scream.

"There we are, little one." The midwife wiped the girl's mouth and then the rest of her tiny body with a mixture of water and wine.

"Let's get you more comfortable," Puah offered.

The queen nodded and lifted her elbows.

Slow and steady, the two students escorted the woman to a nearby couch.

Rania mixed up a soothing patch while Puah wiped the queen's damp brow.

"You did magnificently," she encouraged.

"Here we are," Shiphrah brought over the freshly wrapped baby girl and laid her on her mother's chest.

The scent of oils and spices mixed with fresh life filled Puah's nose. Her heart leapt inside her as she looked down at the rosy cheeks of the girl.

As they watched the baby suckle, Shiphrah asked, "Do we have a name?"

"Neferure."

"Beauty of Ra?" Puah attempted.

"Very good," the queen complimented.

"You've been practicing your Egyptian."

She blushed.

"Neferure is a beautiful name," the mentor added.

"An equally beautiful young one for it to be attached to."

"She is quite striking," Puah agreed.

"Do you think Pharaoh Thutmose II will be disappointed?" the mentor asked.

"He will be all the more ready to try for the next one," she joked as she nuzzled the copper-toned bundle against her cheek. "Besides, Moses is turning into a smart young man. He is outsmarting even his tutors these days. I have no doubt he will be an excellent ruler when the sun rises on his reign."

As if summoned, the strong statured boy of twelve appeared in the doorway. "Mother?"

"Come, my son," Queen Hatshepsut invited. "Come and see your sister."

Moses went to her side and looked down at the baby. "She is lovely." His olive skin was mismatched next to his mother's copper tones. It was obvious to any observer that he wasn't a naturally born son. His nose was far more pointed and his hair was lighter. The look on both their faces though held nothing but love and acceptance.

"She truly is." The proud mother grinned.

"May I hold her?"

"Of course." She extended Neferure out to him. "Be mindful of her head."

He cradled the tightly wrapped newborn in his arms and rocked her slowly. "Hello there. I am Moses."

"A natural brother," the Queen stated.

Puah looked to Moses. It felt like a lifetime since she kissed his newborn forehead. At the same time, it felt like it had just been the day prior. She wondered if that's what it felt like to be a mother. One moment it was as if time stood still and the next as if time slipped through one's fingers like sand.

"Is she well?" Shiphrah asked the woman who guided her and Puah through the massive palace corridor.

Puah's tired feet swelled in her worn sandals. She decided to weave herself a new pair as soon as she could. These were becoming too tight.

It had been two years since the night they helped deliver the new princess into the world. The midwives had made frequent trips to the palace for one thing or another.

"She is well," the maid answered without stopping or turning around.

They made it to an open porch where Queen

Hatshepsut and Moses sat on either side of a small table.

The queen's favorite Senet game board sat on top. The rectangular box, half the size of the table it sat on, had three rows of ten squares and a lioness head carved on the top.

"Ah!" Moses said, moving one of his red jasper pawns across the board.

"Another victory for you." Queen Hatshepsut beamed. "You are getting very good at this game."

He smiled wide.

"Shiphrah. Puah." She turned. "So good to see you both."

"Always a pleasure to serve my Queen." Shiphrah bowed.

"Moses, dear, would you clean up our game and excuse us. I have some things to discuss with these ladies."

"Of course, Mother." He pulled open the side drawer of the box and loaded the ten playing pieces inside.

"Why don't you see if Senenmut will play a few rounds with you?"

He nodded and left with the game safely tucked under his arm.

"He's getting more handsome every day," Puah noted.

"And more headstrong." The queen laughed. "He will make a fine ruler."

"So, why have you called for us today?"

Shiphrah asked.

"I wanted to know if you have thought of anything else for me to try in order to become pregnant again."

"My Queen, as we spoke last time, there are some things that are beyond control."

"We have tried for years," Queen Hatshepsut said, her words weighed down by exhaustion.

"I understand and we've done everything." Shiphrah offered.

"There is nothing left?"

"I'm afraid not, my Queen."

"Moses is such a good brother to his sister, Neferure, but he keeps asking for a brother."

"It is common that a woman never bears any children," Puah interjected. "At least you have Neferure."

"Perhaps Lesser Queen Iset's baby will be a son," Shiphrah suggested.

"Perhaps. If I cannot give my husband a son, maybe his other wife can do so." She looked at the two midwives. "Will you check on Iset for me?"

"We are here to serve." Shiphrah bowed.

"After you are done with her, will you check in on my husband as well?"

"Is he still ill?"

She nodded. "He does not seem well. His magicians are of little help."

"Certainly," Puah answered.

Queen Hatshepsut led the women to the other

side of the Palace where the Lesser Queen Iset resided.

"My Queen," Iset said with a bow as they entered her apartment. "It is an honor."

Queen Iset was a short woman. Her rounded belly poked against her wrapped silk. Though not as beautiful as Hatshepsut, she was still a striking woman and as healthy an Egyptian as Puah had ever seen. She came across more docile and quiet than her higher-ranking counterpart. Where Queen Hatshepsut commanded everyone's attention, Queen Iset was merely content to be in the room.

"These are the best midwives in all Egypt." She motioned to the Hebrews. "I've brought them to look after you."

"That brings me great pleasure."

"May I examine you?" Shiphrah approached.

"Certainly."

After asking several questions and checking on the pregnancy, the older midwife announced, "She's very healthy indeed. Very far along as well."

"Wonderful. Do you think you can stay here until she delivers?"

"We have many who depend on us."

"More than your Queen?"

"No, but-"

"Then the matter is settled. I will make the arrangements." She turned to leave.

"On one condition." She held up her first

finger.

The queen turned back and folded her arms across her chest. "Name it."

"You grant us leave when we need it to perform our duty."

"Do you have other midwives who perform your work when you are assisting patients?" She straightened her back.

"Yes."

"Then have them look after your patients until Iset's delivers."

"My Queen, surely you understand-"

"I understand that you are the best and we deserve nothing but the best."

Shiphrah sighed in defeat. "Of course."

"Splendid. The matter is settled."

"You requested we look in on Pharaoh as well?" Puah interjected.

"Yes, this way." She left instructions with Iset's maidens to prepare a nearby chamber for the Hebrew women. Then she led the midwives to her husband's chambers.

The massive room was big enough for an entire army to occupy comfortably. It was decorated with varying symbols of the sun god Ra. Gold shone in every direction Puah looked.

As they entered the room, the Pharaoh sat dictating to a scribe who sat on the floor. He pressed down on a parchment laid upon a board on the tile. The man was moving the reed in his hand as fast as possible to catch every important word.

"Mighty Pharaoh," Queen Hatshepsut said. "I've brought you some aid."

"I did not request any aid," he growled in a gruff tone from his couch.

"I know, but I have enlisted their help in Iset's pregnancy. While they are staying here to await the arrival of your next child, they have offered their knowledge to help their Pharaoh."

He stared at his wife. "This cannot wait until later?"

"They are available now."

"Very well," he huffed. Then he peered down at the man at his feet. "You are dismissed."

The scribe picked up his writing board and rose. He bowed deeply before leaving the room.

"If I must be interrupted then do get on with it."

"May I examine you?" Shiphrah asked. She leaned her body forward.

"Approach," he said with a nod.

Shiphrah obeyed with Puah following her steps. She looked at his face and noticed the flakey patches she couldn't see from a distance. She stole a quick glance at Hatshepsut before asking, "Would you be so kind as to disrobe?"

"Unspeakable." He rose in a jolt, pushing past the two women, and faced Hatshepsut. "You bring these slaves before me to dishonor me?"

"No. I brought them here to help you. Please," she pleaded. "Do as they request."

He huffed and turned back to them. With a simple movement, he removed his royal robe and allowed it to fall to the ground.

Shiphrah cautiously stepped toward him. The flaky patches covered most of his skin and the places where there were no patches were scarred. "And your headdress."

He shot a dirty look at his Queen.

"Please?" Puah added.

He lifted his large headpiece and held it to his side.

Shiphrah noticed patches where no hair grew and the hair that was on his head was thinning. She looked back over his bare arms and legs. He had little to no muscle. "How long have you had these problems?"

"They have grown worse over the past few years. I do not remember exactly where it started."

"Does it itch?"

"A great deal."

She saw him twitch.

"Can you help him?" Queen Hatshepsut begged.

"I can mix something to help with the itching."

"I have plenty of lotions for that." He returned his headpiece to its original place.

"I'm afraid that's all I can offer." She spread her palms. "I don't know of any cure for such a skin illness."

"Then you are dismissed," he said. He scooped up his robe and returned it to his body.

They bowed and left with the queen.

"Will you mix up the lotions anyway?" she requested.

"Of course," Shiphrah said. "I'll have them ready quickly. They will help. I just wish I had more to offer."

"I do as well. He has become increasingly harsh in his discomfort."

A few days later, Shiphrah and Puah slept soundly in one of the side chambers of the Lesser Queen Iset.

"Midwives," a maid whispered into the dark room. "She calls for you."

"Grab the bag," Shiphrah instructed with a yawn. "Time to meet our new prince or princess."

As the sun kissed the palace walls, Iset kissed the head of her new baby.

"He's healthy," Shiphrah informed Queen Hatshepsut who had attended the birth.

"A boy?"

"Yes, he looks much like his father."

"How much like?"

"He has his eyes and nose, but not his skin illness if that's what you mean."

She closed her eyes. "Thank Ra."

"I received word." Pharaoh Thutmose II entered the room.

"A son," Queen Hatshepsut informed him. "A healthy son."

"Can I see him?"

Iset held the wrapped bundle up.

Pharaoh stepped over and lifted the baby into his arms. "My son. He will be called Thutmose III."

Puah looked over at Queen Hatshepsut. Light reflected off her watery eyes.

She met the glance of the midwife, shook her head, and left the room.

Her heart broke for the queen. The royal woman had two beautiful children to call her own, but she longed for more.

The young midwife had filled her days and her heart with pregnant women and newborn babies. Being witness to the queen's obvious heartbreak only served to harden the resolve in her soul. If husbands and children brought such ache, she wanted no part of them for herself. She simply wished there was something she could do to help the woman who ruled as Queen over all Egypt, but who lacked power over her own womb.

God of the universe, she prayed silently as she watched the queen's form disappear. *You are the One who opens and shuts the womb. If it be Your will, open Hatshepsut's. I know she doesn't honor You, but perhaps a miracle might be the thing to reach her.*

Someone stepped into her path. She blinked a

few times before she recognized Moses standing in the doorway. In two years he had grown from a lanky boy to a person well on his way into manhood. His shoulders and chest were broadening. The sun had tanned his olive complexion into deeper tones.

Though almost as tall as she, he stretched up on his tiptoes to see inside the room.

"A brother," Puah whispered.

His face lit up with joyous excitement.

"Go see him." She stepped aside and motioned with her head.

Chapter 6

"So teach us to number our days..."
-PSALM 90:12

1509 B.C.

"I came as quickly as I heard," Puah said as she slowly entered the princess' chamber.

Queen Hatshepsut knelt beside a large bed in the room. "I am glad you are here," she said without turning around. "Though I wish it were under different circumstances."

"You know I'm always ready to serve, my Queen."

"I was sorry to hear of your mentor's recent passing. Shiphrah was a dear woman. I believe, in a different life, we could have been great friends."

"She was an incredible woman." She edged closer. "Taught me everything I know."

"I had hoped as much."

As she took another few steps, she saw five-year-old Neferure laying in the bed. "What service can I provide today?"

"I have called for every magician and physician who was brave enough to step foot in the palace." Hatshepsut rubbed her daughter's hand. "None of them have been able to help her."

Puah noticed the girl's skin was paler than the last time she saw her. A damp rag lay across her forehead and her skin was soaked with sweat. "A fever?"

The queen nodded.

"How long?"

"Days."

"What have they tried?" She looked at a nearby table covered with bottles and bowls.

"Everything." The queen buried her face in the sheets and wept.

The midwife went over to the table and smelled the different mixtures. Then she returned to the bedside. "May I?" She extended her palm toward the princess.

Queen Hatshepsut looked up and wiped her face. "Of course."

She gently removed the rag and placed her hand on the girl's forehead. "She's very warm."

"Is there anything you can do?"

"Tell me how this started." She replaced the rag.

"She was playing when she began to cough and told me she was tired. I laid her down to rest and when I went to check on her later, she was sweating and her skin was like fire. I called the magicians and that started the rotations of people trying to help. When the last one left this morning, I thought maybe you could…"

"My specialty is birth and babies. I don't know what I can…" She shrugged.

"Please help. You are all I have left. And she is my baby."

She twisted her mouth. "We need to get her fever down. Have them draw fresh water from the springs quickly."

Queen Hatshepsut sent her servants to work.

In no time, they had prepared a bath to Puah's detailed instructions.

She lifted the girl in her arms who stirred ever so slightly. "Shh, my young Princess. I've got a hold of you." She carried her over to the bath. "Help me undress her."

Hatshepsut assisted her and they lowered the girl into the waiting water.

"Hold her head up," Puah encouraged as she poured a mixture into the water and then rubbed another on the girl's skin. "I don't know if any of this will help, but at least we can try."

"I am grateful for your attempts."

"If you don't mind, I'd like to pray."

"I have been praying to every god and goddess I can think of."

"I know One you haven't tried yet." She continued to rub the girl's skin while she prayed, "Lord, God of the universe. You are so mighty in all Your ways. If it be in Your will, restore health to this young one. She is much loved by her family. If You see fit to heal her, do so in Your divine wisdom."

"I have always loved the way you Hebrews pray. You talk to your Deity like he is a friend. A powerful friend, but a friend none the less."

"Have them change the sheets and let's get her out."

The two women carefully lifted the small girl out of the water and robed her in a light dress.

Puah carried her back to the freshly cleaned bed. "There we are."

"Mother?" Princess Neferure whimpered.

"I am here." The queen grasped her hand. "Right here."

"It felt like I was swimming in the Nile." The young girl half smiled.

"Puah helped me give you a bath to try to get rid of your fever."

"Puah?"

"Here, my Princess." She took the girl's other hand.

"Is Mother going to have another baby?"

She looked at Hatshepsut, who dipped her head. "No, dear one. I'm afraid not."

Neferure's crooked smile faded. "I was so hoping for a sister to play with."

"You have your older brother, Moses, and young Thutmose III is growing bigger every day."

"I know, but they are boys and I really want a sister."

"I know you do." Queen Hatshepsut laughed.

"Will you play with me, Puah?"

"Of course, my Princess. I'd be happy to, but we need to get you better first."

"I'm sick?"

"Yes," she answered. "For many days now."

"Mother?"

"Yes?"

"Will you play with us too?"

"Of course." Tears streamed down her cheeks. "We shall play anything you like."

"Can we play after I sleep?" Neferure closed her eyes. "I am very tired."

"Rest, sweet one." The queen kissed her forehead.

Princess Neferure's breaths steadied.

"She looks more peaceful."

"You look exhausted. You should get some rest too. I'd be happy to stay with her." She slid into the large bed, careful not to rouse the sleeping princess.

"I am quite tired, but I would rather stay with her." Queen Hatshepsut slipped in on the other side of her daughter. She adjusted herself to lay on her side in order to watch the girl. "She looks so much like a young goddess when she sleeps."

Puah stretched out on her back and closed her eyes. Soothing scents of the lotions filled her nostrils and cradled her to sleep.

When Puah opened her eyes, the chamber was dark. She was unsure how long she had slept. Turning her head to the side, she saw the form of Princess Neferure in the darkness and Queen Hatshepsut sleeping on the other side. She gently reached over and placed her palm just above the girl's mouth and under her nose. She felt nothing.

"My Queen," she whispered.

The other woman stirred and lifted herself to look over her daughter.

"I'm afraid that…"

"No," the queen whispered. She put her hand on the girl's forehead. "She is no longer warm. That means she is well."

She moved her hand to the girl's cheek. "She's cold, my Queen."

"Neferure, wake up!" the queen shouted as she shook the little girl. "Wake up!"

"She's gone." Tears streamed down her cheeks and she wiped them away with her shoulder. She reached over and put her hand on the queen's arm.

"No." She jerked her hand away. "As her queen, I order her to rise."

"As her mother… let her rest."

"But when we laid down, she looked better. She was speaking to us."

"Remember that. Not as she lays now, but the joyful playfulness. Envision her swimming in the Nile like she imagined herself."

Queen Hatshepsut laid herself over her daughter and wept openly.

She rose and joined her on the other side of the bed. She held her tight until they both ran out of tears.

"I don't understand death," Queen Hatshepsut whispered into Puah's arm.

"Neither do I." She tightened her grip on the woman and lifted her up to God in prayer. *You give and take away, Lord. Bless Your name.*

Six years later, another death haunted the palace.

"The falcon is flown to heaven and Queen Hatshepsut is arisen in his place," the voice of an aide echoed off the walls of the palace complex.

Puah stood with many others in the streets of Peru-nefer. The news of Pharaoh Thutmose II's death had come to her like many messages, on the tongues of neighborhood women.

While her people in the land of Goshen rejoiced, she wept for Queen Hatshepsut who had lost her only daughter and now her husband. She had become close with the royal woman and visited the palace as often as she could.

The queen's maiden approached. "Go to her." Her normally warm smile was gone from her lips. Tears reddened her eyes and wet her face.

She searched the woman's eyes. "Has she called?"

"No." The woman bowed her head and shook it slightly. "But she needs you."

Picking up the hem of her dress, she flew on her tiptoes into the palace and toward the queen's chamber.

When she reached the doorway, she slowed. "Queen Hatshepsut," she called.

"Come."

Upon entering, she found the woman standing beside one of her tables.

The royal woman picked up a bottle and emptied some of its contents into her hand before rubbing it all over her fingers.

"I could mix you up a better lotion if your hands are still bothering you."

"This comes all the way from Persia," Queen Hatshepsut insisted. "It does just fine."

Puah nodded, not really knowing what else to offer.

"You have no doubt heard of my husband's passing by now."

"Along with all Egypt, I have. We mourn your loss. He was a good Pharaoh."

"He was a weak man," she hissed under her breath.

"My Queen?"

"Disregard that." She moved to sit on one of the large couches. "I am sure you did not come to discuss medicine or my dead husband."

"I came to see how you are faring."

"Well enough." She picked up the deep blue sash that hung from her waist and ran it through her fingers. "Though I could use your help with a delicate matter."

"My Queen certainly has better resources than I."

"I do." She softened. "But I know you will be honest with me. Your mentor treated my family with love and grace. You, yourself, have treated us no less."

Puah bowed her head. "I'm but a humble servant."

"I didn't get the chance to treat Shiphrah as a friend. I am hoping to rectify that by extending confidentiality to you."

She lifted her head and made eye contact.

"My husband's death leaves a vacant throne. My beloved Moses has reached his twenty-second year, but still has much to learn." She straightened to sit up tall. "I'm not sure if the people are ready to accept him. Until such time as I feel he is ready, I will no longer hold the title of Queen Hatshepsut. From this day forward, I will be taking the title of Pharaoh Hatshepsu. It is my duty to unite our people."

She resisted the urge to disagree. "I don't know what I can offer as assistance."

"You have much knowledge from which our

people can benefit. I seek your wisdom."

"If it be your request, I'll do my best."

"Good." She rose. "We have much to plan."

Chapter 7

"And it came to pass in those days, when Moses was grown, that he went out unto his brethren,"
-EXODUS 2:11

1495 B.C.

Puah shifted her weight on her bare feet. She had been in such a rush this morning that she forgot to tie on a pair of sandals. The cool tile was a welcome relief to her old, sweaty feet.

"Are you feeling better today?" Puah asked.

"Somewhat," Pharaoh Hatshepsu answered as she applied lotion to her hands.

The routine of visiting the palace every day to adhere to the commands of Pharaoh before she was allowed to see her patients was beginning to wear on her.

"I seem to have good days and bad. Also, I am having another irritation."

"Oh?"

"Here." The woman took off her headcloth

and untied the ribbon at the top of her head which released the strap of her false beard. She pointed to her chin.

She moved closer. "Yes. There does seem to be some redness. Possibly from your beard."

Hatshepsu rubbed the spot. "Is there anything you can do?"

"I would suggest to keep the area clean and give the skin time to rest."

Pharaoh straightened. The line of her mouth almost disappeared with disapproval.

"But seeing as how that doesn't please you, I can give you some lotion to rub on at night when you remove the beard. That should help."

"Wonderful."

"Mighty Pharaoh," Senenmut said, entering the chamber with a deep bow. "The sailors have returned from their voyage."

"Excellent." She tied her beard back on and replaced her headcloth. "Let us go welcome them."

"I should excuse myself," Puah requested. "I have many women to visit."

"They can wait. Your Pharaoh wishes for you to see the many gifts that have been brought from afar."

"Of course. As you wish."

"Call for Moses to join us," she ordered a waiting attendant.

Once they reached the throne room, Pharaoh

Hatshepsu sat on her golden throne. Her first act as ruler had been to have a custom seat made to replace her husband's. This one was covered in lioness carvings and slightly raised to make her appear even taller than he had sat.

Puah stood by to witness the exchange but kept in sight of Pharaoh as to please the royal woman.

"Moses," Pharaoh beamed as the man entered the room with a deep bow. She extended her arms to him.

He approached and embraced her. "It is good to see you this beautiful morning."

"I am so pleased to see you as well." She held him out to arm's length. "You remember Puah?" She waved toward her.

"Yes. The midwife." He nodded. "Greetings." Puah bowed.

"She is such a gifted medicine woman." Pharaoh bragged.

"Are you still feeling ill?" Moses' face scrunched with study as he looked over her.

"Better. Thanks in large part to Puah."

"I am grateful for your care of my mother."

"It's my honor to serve, my Prince."

"I have a special surprise for you." Pharaoh pointed to the group of men waiting before the throne.

"Mighty Pharaoh," a weary sailor approached. "We have returned with many rewards from the land of Punt." He motioned to the men standing behind him.

The group brought forward large trees with their roots carefully wrapped in cloth and placed in baskets.

"As you have requested, mighty Pharaoh." He walked over to the nearest tree and rubbed its leaves. "Thirty-one myrrh trees."

"You have done well." She smiled toward Moses. "Does this gift please you?"

Moses looked at the trees and back to his mother. "I do not understand."

"Thirty-one trees. One for each year of your life."

"I see."

"I'm going to have them planted in the courts of Djeser-Djeseru."

"We have also brought frankincense." The sailor called for the other baskets.

"Bring some here," Pharaoh requested.

A maiden retrieved a bundle from the men and brought it to her.

"You have all done well." She rose and invited Puah to follow her with a graceful movement of her hand.

When the two were back in her private chamber, Hatshepsu unwrapped the gift.

"I want to show you something."

Puah watched as Pharaoh placed some of the frankincense in a wide bowl. She took it over to a burning fire and charred the hard resin until it changed into a dark liquid. Bringing it back to her table, she allowed the substance to cool for a few moments.

She took a sharpened reed and dipped it into the liquid. Raising the stick, she ever so softly swept the material under her eye. Dipping again, she stroked another line on her upper eyelid right above her lashes. Then she turned to Puah. "What do you think?"

Puah tilted her head. "It makes your eyes stand out."

"It is to help with the sun. This way our people can work longer on sunny days without straining their eyes."

"That's incredible." She stepped closer.

"I thought you would enjoy it."

Nearly a decade later, Puah stood in Pharaoh Hatshepsu's private chamber as she did every morning. Often it was to provide medical advice. More often than not, it was to provide a humble ear.

"Yesterday I offered Moses the title of Pharaoh," the regal woman explained.

"Wonderful news."

"It would have been if he had accepted."

Pharaoh rose and walked around the room.

Her royal robes glided across the floor with her movements. "Many men strive their whole lives to capture such a title. I thought he was finally ready. Yet, he willingly walks away from the biggest offer that could be given." She stopped in front of Puah. "I have heard rumors."

"About Moses." She looked at her well-worn sandals.

"Are they true?"

The midwife swallowed hard. "They are true."

"How could he?"

"I'm not sure." She shifted the weight on her feet. "He is such an incredible man."

"How could he kill?"

"That's the account."

"Tell me." Pharaoh sat on her couch.

"He went to observe our people's bondage and witnessed an Egyptian beating a Hebrew slave. In a rage, he struck the taskmaster with a death blow. Then he covered the body in the sand."

"Oh, Moses," she spoke to the man who was not there. "Why would you lash out so?"

"When he returned," she went on. "He saw two Hebrews fighting with each other and he tried to intervene. When he attempted to help settle the argument, they told them they witnessed him kill the Egyptian."

"This mess is my fault." She held her head in her hands. "My father set taskmasters over your people to keep them under control. He feared your numbers. I feared for my people if I set all of you free." She looked into Puah's face. "I got so busy showing strength so as to keep the favor of my people, I did not bother making changes to protect yours. The taskmasters have become drunk with their power. If I had set things right, Moses would not have murdered that man."

"We should have him killed for murder," Thutmose III entered the room.

Puah noticed how much the young boy of ten resembled his father. It was like watching time replay itself. He marched into the room and stood right in front of his mother. He was only half her height, but he held his head high and his back as straight as an arrow.

"It is our law," he demanded, trying to make his voice deeper than it would normally go.

"He is family." She rose to stand over him. "We can forgive such a transgression." The queen reached to cup her son's small chin.

The boy pulled away in disgust. "Father would have brought justice."

"Your father is not here and you are not old enough to judge such matters." She turned to Puah. "Is he really gone?"

"Yes, he set out in the middle of the night. He didn't even leave word with his family which way he was heading."

"Very well." She folded her hands together in a delicate manner. "We will not give chase."

"Mighty Pharaoh-"

She held up a hand to her step-son. "Let the gods deal with him."

He huffed and stormed out of the room.

The royal woman sank back into her chair. "I cannot believe he is truly gone. I had such high hopes of him being a great Pharaoh. The work on his tomb is halfway complete. He was to lay as one of our great kings after a mighty rule."

Puah gazed over the queen. The woman looked as heartsick as any she had seen. Her eyes were reddened with lack of sleep. Her robe was tied in haste and left to hang as it was.

"Is there anything I can do?" she offered

Pharaoh looked up at her. "Can you pray to your God to bring my son back?"

She nodded. With a sincere wish and a silent prayer, she longed for Moses to return as well. If left in the hands of the angry young man who had just left the room, she knew her people's path would be a rough one. If Moses returned, they might have a chance to thrive.

Chapter 8

"And it came to pass in the process of time, that the king of Egypt died:"
-EXODUS 2:23

1457 B.C.

Puah's tight back pulled as she walked toward the palace complex in Peru-nefer. Eight and a half decades had been kind to her, but time has a way of catching up with everyone sooner or later. She dreamed of starting life renewed as the twelve-year-old girl who went knocking on Shiphrah's gate. Perhaps she should have waited a few more years to see if any prospective husband ever came calling.

Then she recounted all the fresh faces of new life she had cradled in her arms. She held up her hands. They were wrinkled and cracked with age. Scars marred her once smooth skin. Her fingers bent at the knuckles so that they never fully straightened. They were so different from the skin of the newborns she eased into the world. Though that's something she wouldn't trade for all the husbands in the world.

It had become increasingly necessary to ask her Hebrew apprentice, Eliora, for more and more help when it came to preparing food or cleaning the house. Her Egyptian student, Layla, had made herself useful in a different way by working with the patients and seeing those patients further out.

Puah appreciated both women in their unique ways. She didn't know if any Egyptian women would want to be under her teaching. Many divisions had occurred over the past few decades and new ones revealed themselves each passing week. Layla had accepted the position and seemed open enough to learning, even from a Hebrew.

Midwifery was one thing. It was Puah's passion. It was why she got up in the morning. Taking care of daily chores was another thing altogether. Her young student had been thrilled with the added responsibilities. Her heart was so full of willingness to serve that she didn't even hesitate with each request.

Puah remembered herself as a bright young woman ready to learn her duties under her mentor.

Shiphrah.

Only one of many names that brought memories flooding back to her.

Her dear mentor had taught her with grace

and compassion. She had instructed her in the ways of her trade as well as the ways of life. When it came down to it, Shiphrah had become a second mother to her. She had taken Puah under her broad wing and guided her to be the woman she was today. Her mentor's simple ideas and bold passion stirred something in her that she could never quite explain.

She missed her dearly.

Her heavy heart weighed down her steps.

To date, she had seen the rise and fall of three Pharaohs. Two had been men striving to expand Egypt into new territories. One had been a woman who helped Egypt thrive within its own borders.

Hatshepsut.

The woman who started out as a tolerance had grown a special place in Puah's heart.

She wept for weeks after the announcement rang from the palace complex, "The falcon is flown to heaven and Pharaoh Thutmose III is arisen in his place."

Partly because the two had become inseparable in the twenty years she ruled as Pharaoh. They had become as close as royalty and servant were allowed. Each knowing their place, yet respecting the other as a valued confidant.

She had longed to visit the vast complex the woman had built in the south for herself, but her old body had only been able to make the trip once since the Pharaoh's passing. It was just too far for her to travel alone.

The other part was primarily because of the step-son who replaced her. For the last twenty-five years, Puah had barely stepped foot in the palace under the new Pharaoh. He had little patience for her people and even less need for a midwife. He held firm to his own magicians and aides to solve any problem within his walls.

This made it even more of a surprise when she was summoned that morning to arrive at the palace complex. Her heart feared an edict like the one she disobeyed as a young midwife so long ago. Shiphrah had taken the lead in the plan that had saved countless Hebrew boys. She didn't know if she had the strength or stamina to fight this Pharaoh.

Her body ached and her mind missed the faces of all who had gone before. Her partner apprentice, Rania, had a long practice as a midwife in the south until her death. She thought about all pregnant women and children she had seen grow old and pass on. Her heart hurt with loneliness. She missed those who had gone through shared experiences with her. She missed chatting about the old days.

Eliora's bright personality and thirst for knowledge had kept her going through the darkest of days. The young girl's spirit had renewed Puah's passion when she most wanted to give in. If it had not been for the younger woman, she would have longed for the welcoming arms of peaceful rest that awaited her on the other side of this world.

"Do they speak Hebrew?" Eliora's question interrupted Puah's distant thoughts.

She hadn't noticed that her student had been holding a one-sided conversation the entire time they had been walking until that moment.

"Many of them study numerous languages, but they expect you to speak Egyptian when you stand before them."

"I hope I won't have to do any speaking." She frowned. "I haven't been practicing like you asked."

"If you're going to serve their people, you need to respect them."

"I'll do better." She beamed. "I promise."

Puah tried to straighten her limp.

"Would you like to stop and let me help you stretch that out?"

"No." She shook her head. "I don't like to keep Pharaohs waiting." She pushed through the pain. "I'll manage."

When they came upon the massive gates, the guards stepped aside to give them passage.

Puah expertly managed the twists and turns of the long corridors. She had walked the halls so many times she could probably do it without sight. With her eyes dimming as they were, it wouldn't be long before she could try.

"Mighty Pharaoh," she said with a bow as they entered the throne room. "May you live forever."

Pharaoh Thutmose III sat upon a golden throne marked with the god of the sun. Puah noticed that he didn't look like his father at the same age. That was a good thing in terms of health. Where his father had lost muscle and grew skin lesions all over his body, this Thutmose's skin shone a brilliant bronze. Exposed muscles rippled under his minimal clothing and extravagant ornamentation. He was a perfect picture of power.

"Puah, the midwife," an aide introduced.

"The what?"

"The midwife, your Excellence." The aide adjusted his neck collar. "The Hebrew woman your wife requested."

"Very well." He waved them off without much of a glance. "Send them to her."

"This way," one of the massive men Pharaoh employed as a guard motioned.

Puah and Eliora bowed and followed the man.

"Whew!" the younger student said in a whispered Hebrew tongue.

"Keep your guard up," her mentor ordered in a lower tone.

"I'll take them from here," a maiden spoke to the guard as they neared a side apartment. She was a simple woman, though beautiful, with kind eyes.

He gave a slight nod before turning around and marching away.

"I'm pleased you have accepted my lady's invitation." She bent a little and spread her arms. Her white silk robe and turquoise cat amulet indicated to Puah that she must be one of the queen's top servants. Every Queen she had ever known wanted the women around her to be dressed in their best at all times.

"I'm afraid we don't understand why exactly we've been called upon," Puah's tongue smoothed over the Egyptian words.

"Queen Satiah is experiencing some discomfort in her pregnancy that our aides have not been able to calm."

"Oh?"

"Yes. There are rumors that your Hebrew midwives are much more knowledgeable in this area. And that you, in particular, are a friend to the palace."

"We are eager to serve."

"I know that will please the Queen." She waved her delicate hands toward the entrance. "This way, please."

Puah and Eliora followed closely behind the woman as she led them into the queen's chamber.

"My Queen," the woman announced as she came upon her mistress. "I have gathered more aid for you."

Queen Satiah reclined on a large couch. The curve of the piece of furniture cradled the heavily pregnant woman perfectly. Golden lion's paws stuck out of the legs of the couch as if it were ready to pounce on its prey at any given moment. An orange-red carnelian pillar amulet hung heavy around her neck.

"Are you suffering from back pains?" Puah inquired.

"I am." The queen straightened as best she could. "How did you know?" She glanced at her maid, assuming the woman had given away the details of the visit.

The woman spread her hands and shrugged.

"I've spent much time around Egyptians and I am familiar with your practices." Puah pointed to the necklace. "The symbol you wear there is often used to help alleviate back pain and promote stability to its wearer."

She rubbed her fingers over the smooth gemstone. "You are as intelligent as they claim."

"Can you tell me what other issues you've been dealing with?"

She rubbed the sides of her stomach. "Tightness on either side that doesn't seem to have a rhythm."

"Comes and goes when you move?"

She nodded.

"I believe you are suffering from false labor."

"Is it serious?"

"No. It's simply your body's way of getting ready for the real thing."

"Is there anything that can be done?"

"There are lots of things to help." She put her bag down and sat near the couch. "First is to make sure you're drinking plenty of liquids."

"I can see to that," the maiden added.

"You can also try a warm bath. That usually helps the muscles calm down."

The queen lifted her head to motion her servant. "Have one drawn."

"Straight away." She left to fulfill the request.

"Once you're done with that, I'd also like to try a massage."

"That sounds divine."

"My student and I can show your servant some techniques so she can help when we are not available."

"Wonderful."

After a long soak in warm water and an instructional massage, Puah noticed the more relaxed face of the Queen as she lay on her couch. "Feeling better?"

"Much." She smiled.

"How long have you been suffering?"

"A few days."

"How far along are you?"

"I do not know exactly."

"It won't be long. I'd say by the end of the month or sooner."

"I am truly grateful for your help."

"It's my pleasure to serve."

"I would like to reward you."

Puah held up her hand. "That's not necessary, my Queen."

"Of course it is." She waved over her maiden. "Nailah, fetch that box of jewelry from my bedchamber."

She bowed deeply and hurried to retrieve the item. Upon her return, she placed a gold box on the queen's lap.

Queen Satiah lifted the lid and placed it next to her leg. Her fingertips danced over the array of colors inside.

"Ah," she indicated. "Here we are." She lifted a simple necklace out of the pile and held it up.

Polished red jasper caught a few glints of the rays of sunlight that poured into the room through the wide windows. The gemstone had been expertly carved into a seated lioness.

Puah's eyes watered as a memory flooded her mind. The same necklace had hung around Queen Hatshepsut's neck when they first met. It was a gift from her father when she turned thirteen. She wore it with poise on many occasions.

The Queen extended the necklace towards her.

She bowed her head and intertwined her fingers. "It's not right for me to accept such a lavish gift."

"I insist. You have pleased your Queen and I seek to reward such acts." She stretched her arm further.

"Thank you." Puah clasped the charm firmly in the palm of her hand and closed her fingers around it. The cool stone felt good against her warm skin. She pulled her fist in tight to her chest. "If there is anything else I can assist with, please call on me."

"I might take you up on that offer."

She bowed and left the apartment.

When they stepped into the open city streets, Eliora spoke first, "That was a beautiful gift."

Puah nodded.

"Aren't you going to put it on?"

She stopped. She still held her tightened fist to her chest. "I couldn't wear such a thing. What would my patients think?"

"The Egyptians walk around layered in fine jewelry and lavish garments. If it's truly a gift, then you should wear it proudly."

She opened her hand to reveal the somber face of the flaming jasper lioness. "You think?"

"Yes."

The young woman lifted the chain from Puah's hand and extended it over her head. The charm dropped down and dangled perfectly on her chest.

"It suits you."

"It's stunning." She ran her fingers over the gemstone feeling the slight variations in the etchings. "I never thought I'd own such a fine piece of jewelry."

Chapter 9

*"Now there arose up a new king over Egypt,
which knew not Joseph."*
-EXODUS 1:8

Three weeks later, a loud knock at the gate interrupted Eliora's sweeping. "I'll see to it," she called.

She straightened and put the hand broom in the corner before going to the gate.

Puah stepped to the doorway leading from the main room into the open courtyard. She leaned upon the post.

When Eliora opened the door, a young guard clad in royal colors stood tall.

"I have a message from the palace," he said.

"Hoshea?" Puah crossed the courtyard and came to the gate.

A Hebrew boy she had held in her hands almost twenty years before stood broad-shouldered and brave before her.

"Puah." He bowed. "It is good to see you well."

"And you." She bowed back. "Your mother mentioned you had been selected to train with Pharaoh's army. She wore a smile as proud as a warrior wears a battle scar speaking about you."

His sun-kissed cheeks turned pink and he tipped his head with a nod.

"Is your father well?"

He cleared his throat. "Yes. Thank you."

"Ah-hem," Eliora's noise beside them caught Puah's attention.

"My apologies." She waved to her apprentice. "Hoshea, son of Nun, I'd like to introduce one of my students, Eliora."

"A pleasure." He bowed with a bright smile before straightening and adjusting his neck collar. "I wish this was a social visit."

"Oh?" she asked.

"I've been sent to escort you to the palace."

"Pharaoh?"

"Not that serious." He relaxed. "Queen Satiah actually. She seeks your presence at once."

"Of course." She squared her shoulders. "Let us just grab a bag and we'll be ready."

Eliora followed her to their supplies. She grabbed a knife to put in the bag but dropped it.

Puah reached for her shaking hand. "Are you unwell?"

The younger woman met her eyes. "I don't know what's wrong with me."

She placed an open palm on her cheek. "You're

flushed. Maybe you should stay here. I'm sure I can handle-"

"No!" she shouted.

The mentor pulled her hand back.

"I'm sorry." She stole a quick glance toward the courtyard and then back to Puah. "I mean, no, I'm well." She returned to filling the bag.

Puah looked to the gate and smiled. Hoshea still stood there waiting for them.

"What do you think she wants?" Eliora asked.

"I don't know." She answered, pretending not to notice the change of subject. "Maybe her false labor is increasing?"

"Maybe I'll get a necklace this time?" She giggled.

Puah swatted the girl with the rag in her hand. "Pack your own bag and let's find out."

"Do you think we should wait for Layla to return?"

She shook her head. "If there's one thing I've learned it's-"

"Never keep a Pharaoh waiting." She smiled wide.

"There is still much for you to learn, young one. But I'm glad to know you've been listening."

The two women hurried toward Peru-nefer with their escort.

Eliora made sure to keep a step behind her mentor.

Puah played with the idea that it was either to

simply show respect or to keep herself from the handsome guard that led them. Duty kept her from discovering the truth, along with the present company.

"I'll leave you here," Hoshea said with a bow as they passed through the entrance and toward the queen's maiden.

Puah noticed Eliora's gaze followed his long stride as he disappeared.

"Appearing as requested." She bowed toward Nailah.

Deep blue beads of lapis lazuli lined the servant's neck and rolled with her movements. "The Queen will be pleased to see you again."

"Is she well?" Eliora asked, trying her Egyptian.

The maiden tilted her head at the young girl. "She believes her pains are more regular and asked me to fetch Puah to attend to her birth."

"It will be an honor to assist," she offered.

"This way." She glided down the tiled hallway.

"You've been practicing," Puah whispered in Hebrew into the ear of Eliora.

The student beamed.

"Keep up the good work."

"The women you requested," Nailah announced as they entered the bedchamber.

Queen Satiah lay on her bed. Gold rods shone bright with matching gazelle hoof feet. Her head was delicately supported by the curved wooden headboard. White linens covered the woven mattress and lotus flowers decorated the wide footboard.

Puah thought of the worn straw mat wrapped in the corner of her home waiting to be uncurled when she returned to lay her head down that night.

What it must be like to sleep in a proper bed for just one night.

"You said by the end of the month," the queen's words invaded her thoughts.

"So I did." She smiled. "Would you mind if we have a look at you?"

"That is why I called." She tensed.

Layla arrived late into the evening upon hearing from a neighbor that Puah and Eliora had been summoned to the palace.

As the oil lamps were lit in the private chamber, Puah instructed the servants and her apprentices to set up a birthing stool.

"You can't expect our Queen to give birth like a slave," Nailah protested.

"Women are women. This is one of the most effective ways to give birth. She has sought my wisdom in this regard and I intend to perform my duties to the best of my abilities. I'm sure she expects you to do the same."

The servant turned away with a flip of her robe and a stifled grunt.

"Soon?" Queen Satiah gasped between

breaths.

"Soon." Puah nodded. "Let's get you into place."

The younger women eased the queen over to the stones.

"That's it, my Queen. Baby is coming," she encouraged the woman.

She panted and bore down.

"He's here!" Puah shared. "A boy!"

"Wonderful." She gasped for air. "Pharaoh will be so pleased."

"Look at him." She held the wiggling boy up. "He's got your eyes."

The midwife set to work wiping the baby down with a mix of water and wine, rubbing him with prepared oils, and then wrapping him in fresh linens.

"Hello there, my son." The royal woman accepted the boy from Puah and laid him on her chest. While he suckled, she held his head full of dark hair.

"Has Pharaoh decided a name?" Eliora inquired.

"Amenemhat."

"He doesn't wish to keep his family name going?"

"He wishes to erase them from our history. If he could change his own name, he would. At least he can start by giving our son a proper name."

"His father and grandfather did much to

increase the lands of Egypt," Puah voiced. "They were mighty men who are honored by your people. And Pharaoh Hatshepsu. She brought peace to the land and dramatically increased trade."

"She was a lunatic and nothing more than a power-hungry woman," Pharaoh Thutmose III's deep-voiced boomed from behind them.

"Mighty Pharaoh," Puah said with a low bow. "I didn't mean-"

He held up a hand. "I do not wish to spend any more time wasting my breath discussing that woman." He waved her off as he passed. "I have come to see my child."

"A son, Mighty Pharaoh," Queen Satiah reported. "A strong child."

Chapter 10

"And Moses took his wife and his sons, and set them upon an ass, and he returned to the land of Egypt:"
-EXODUS 4:20

1447 B.C.

Puah wiped some perspiration from her forehead. The heat was rising to its pinnacle late in the month of Av. Her heart broke thinking about the men laboring out in the feverish temperatures to build cities for Pharaoh. The women also toiled day and night to serve the people of Egypt. Her guild of midwives was fortunate enough to live and serve free, but her people weren't.

"Who are we visiting today?" Eliora called over her shoulder while packing a bag.

"An Egyptian woman named Sofh," she answered from the other room. "She believes she is pregnant with her first child."

"How exciting."

The two women made their way into the city of Memphis towards the home of the waiting woman.

"Please, enter." A servant girl bowed and waved them in. "My lady is expecting you."

"Greetings." Puah bowed as they approached the reclined woman. "I'm Puah and this is one of my apprentices, Eliora." She waved to the younger woman.

"Aria, these are the best midwives you could find?" the ornately dressed woman spoke over their heads to her waiting servant.

"Yes, my lady. They are the most highly recommended midwives in all of Egypt."

"But they are dressed so humbly." She eyed the two Hebrew women for a long time. "And they smell."

Puah felt heat rise in her cheeks with a mix of anger and embarrassment. "I can assure you, Mistress, we are very clean and honored to be assisting you with your pregnancy."

"Let me see your hands," she demanded.

The two midwives stepped closer with outstretched hands.

"Callouses. I should have known. Filthy Hebrew slaves."

"If you are unhappy, my lady, I can fetch new midwives," Aria offered.

She searched the two women standing in front of her again before answering, "They are already here. We shall see how good they are." She waved off her servant. "Next time." Sofh narrowed her gaze toward the midwives. "Don't come into my home smelling like cattle."

"Yes, Mistress." Puah bit her tongue. "May I ask you a few questions?"

Sofh sighed and rolled herself onto her back. "If you must."

"When was your last bleeding?"

"Six weeks ago, and I'm terribly miserable. I haven't been able to keep down any food."

The midwife eyed the bowls overflowing with fresh fruit on the table next to them. "Would you mind if I examine you?"

Sofh wrinkled her nose. "If you go wash first." She pointed to the doorway.

"Of course," she said with a bow and stepped into the next room.

Eliora followed. "I'd like to give that woman a piece of my mind," she spoke in Hebrew through tight lips.

"Silence." Puah placed her finger over her lips. "We are guests in her home. It is not right to speak about the lady of the house in such a manner."

"She's so disrespectful."

"Not in her eyes." The mentor scrubbed her hands in a waiting water basin. "All Hebrews are slaves to these people, whether we truly are or not. I wouldn't expect her to treat us any differently."

"We are not here to please her, we are here to

ensure a safe and healthy pregnancy so she may hold her child."

"We are here to serve just as any other servant." She washed her hands again. "Now, wash up and help me."

The women returned to examine Sofh.

"You seem very healthy," Puah reported.

"You'd expect anything less?" The pregnant woman huffed.

"I'd like to come by in another few weeks and see how you are doing?"

"That will be-" Sofh started, but gagged on her next words. She bent over a nearby bowl and heaved several times.

Aria rushed in and held a cloth to her mistress' forehead.

"That will subside with time," Puah explained.

The Egyptian woman glared up at her before starting another round of dry heaves.

"I'll leave a mixture with your servant. Try drinking a few sips in the morning when you rise and it should help."

When Sofh collapsed back onto her couch, Aria followed the women to the door.

"Let the roots steep in some warm water for a few moments. Remember, only let her sip on it," the mentor instructed.

Aria nodded.

"If it doesn't get better before I return, call for me and I'll bring her some other herbs."

"Thank you."

"Aria!" Sofh shouted.

"You best go," Eliora suggested. "We can see ourselves out."

The young girl bowed and rushed back to her mistress.

"You can head back to the house and help Layla," Puah said as they walked along. "I have another stop I'd like to make alone."

"Are you sure?"

She nodded. "I'll return before dark."

"If you wish." The younger woman turned herself toward the direction of their home.

Puah wandered the streets of Avaris in search of the home of Aaron. When she finally found the right building, she entered the large courtyard and was greeted by his wife, Elisheba. She was a small, humble woman. She liked to keep to herself but lived to serve any guest who entered her home.

"It's good to see you." The midwife met the woman at the gate. "How are those four boys of yours?"

"Very well."

"Wonderful. I'm here to speak with-"

"Elisheba, who was there?" A petite woman came into the courtyard from one of the rooms. She held a wet rag in her hand and her dress was covered in food.

Two young ones hurried past her chasing each other.

"Gershom and Eliezer," she scolded.

The boys stopped in the tracks.

"Go play out back."

They rushed off without another word.

"This is my friend, Puah," Elisheba waved.

Puah bowed.

"She's come for a visit." The woman beamed so wide that it reached her eyes. "She's a wonderful midwife and helped deliver all of my boys." She turned to Puah. "This is my sister-in-law, Zipporah."

"That would make you Moses' wife," Puah figured.

"Yes, it would." The woman put both hands on her broad hips.

"Actually, I'm here to speak with Moses. Is he here?"

Elisheba looked over her shoulder and back to her guest. "How did you know?"

"I take care of women, my dear. They have loose lips when they gather."

"Isn't that the truth." Zipporah smiled and wiped her hand on her apron. "Please, come in." She stepped back into the kitchen area and returned to her tasks.

Puah walked into the common room and placed her bag beside the doorway.

Elisheba followed. "They are in the next room. I can get-"

"That's an outrageous plan," Aaron's voice

carried from the next room with exasperation evident in his tone. The thin veil between the two rooms did little to hide their conversation. "You've been repeating it since I met you in the wilderness."

Moses huffed.

"Of course it is," Miriam said, her voice carrying just as loud from the room. "Have you ever heard God doing anything inside man's strength?"

Aaron shot his sister a dirty look.

"Husband," Elisheba called.

Aaron approached them. He was a massive man. Puah knew that he had spent his youth working in the quarries, but with time they moved him to a position of leadership and less of hard work. The sun had tanned his olive skin dark and the intensive workload had kept him fit.

"This is Puah and she wants to speak with you."

Aaron exchanged a glance with Moses, who had come to stand next to him.

She met eyes with the man she hadn't seen in decades. His face was wrinkled with age and marked with the sands of the desert. His hair was graying at his temples and some flecks showed in his long beard. Bright eyes shone from under shaggy eyebrows. He stood tall and proud. Whatever he had done while gone for the past forty years had kept his physical body in decent shape.

"I don't know if you remember me," Puah started. "I assisted your mother when she gave birth to you. My mentor, Shiphrah, and I organized the midwife network that saved many Hebrew boys under the edict that would have cost you your life."

"Of course." Miriam joined them. "It's good to see you well. And Shiphrah?"

"She died many years ago." She hung her head.

"I'm sure she is enjoying Paradise as we speak."

Miriam's hair was just as dark as Puah remembered. The young girl had grown into a beaming woman. Though older than both of her brothers, she had aged well enough that someone who didn't know the siblings would peg her as the youngest. Being spared from the powerful rays of the Egyptian sun, her olive complexion was clear and bright in comparison to the leather skin of her brothers.

She nodded. "I'm sure God greatly rewarded her faithfulness to Him. She was a brave woman who feared God."

"And you as well."

"Not as brave. I was just young at the time. I knew following God was the right thing to do, but I was a lot more frightened than Shiphrah. She was so sure of herself."

"Yet, you stand before us now?" the sister asked.

"Yes. To speak with Moses."

"Speaking will be a difficulty," Aaron murmured.

She tilted her head. "I don't understand."

"Best I can gather, our brethren in the wilderness speak a different form of our language. It has taken some time to learn to communicate."

"I speak Hebrew and Egyptian. I'm sure I can understand him well enough."

"Why do you seek him?" he questioned with a slight lift of his head.

"I heard he has returned from the wilderness."

"He has."

"I've also heard he will be requesting an audience with Pharaoh." She straightened her shoulders and ignored the aching muscles in her back. "I've heard he wants to request leave to make sacrifices to God."

Aaron looked at his younger brother. "That's what he tells me."

"Then I'm here to offer my assistance."

"You?" he asked. "What help could you offer?"

"I've served the royals on many occasions. I also know Pharaoh will not see you unless you've been called."

"Apparently he has something to get Pharaoh's attention."

"What is it?"

"Rod?" Moses asked his brother.

"Mine?"

He nodded.

Aaron huffed out of the room and returned with his staff. He jammed it into Moses' chest.

Moses handed it back to him and pointed to the ground. "Throw."

He looked at the women around the room.

"Better do as he asks," Miriam suggested.

The brother lifted the rod above his head and pitched it to the ground.

When the stick hit the sandy floor, it transformed into a slithering serpent.

All three women took a step back.

"You get that thing out of our house," Elisheba demanded.

"Retrieve." Moses pointed to the snake.

"Are you mad, brother?" Aaron protested. "It'll bite me."

He simply shook his head and pointed to the serpent.

Aaron edged closer to the snake and quickly reached just behind its head. As soon as his hand touched the skin, it transformed back into a rod. He turned it over and over again, waiting for it to slither once more.

"Do you think that will convince Pharaoh?" Puah wondered.

Moses shrugged.

"When do we try?" Aaron asked. "As the midwife said, you don't just walk into the palace without being summoned."

She rubbed her chin. "Leave that part to me." She retrieved her bag. "Follow me, but let me do the talking."

Aaron shot his brother a glance. "Let the woman speak for us," he joked. "So, I can speak for Moses. So, Moses can speak for God. This is some plan." He folded his arms across his chest and shook his head.

Moses stood by Puah and called over his shoulder toward his brother. "Coming?"

"I don't know what you're getting me into, brother." Aaron kissed his wife and followed the two toward the palace.

Puah stood straight as they approached the guards. "I am Puah, the midwife. I'm here for Queen Satiah."

The two guards stared at Moses and Aaron before exchanging glances.

"No one has called for you," the taller one said.

"I'd hate for you to incur the wrath of Pharaoh if you continue to hold me up from seeing his Great Royal Wife."

"You may enter," the other said. "But they must stay here."

"They need to come with me," she said, leaving hesitation out of her words in the hope she could persuade them.

"Why?"

"Because…" Her normally quick thoughts had come to a standstill in her mind. "Because…"

"Puah?" Queen Satiah's voice echoed off the walls as she approached them.

"My Queen." She bowed.

"Let them pass," the queen ordered.

Each man stepped aside.

"It's wonderful to see you well, my Queen." She kept her voice light and moved so the group would be a few steps away from the royal protection.

"Should I be different?" Queen Satiah examined the two men with the midwife.

"I need an audience with you." Puah looked over her shoulder at the guards who stood nearby. "A private audience."

"I see." The royal woman stretched her neck to address the soldiers, "You are dismissed."

The two men marched back to their post at the gate.

Queen Satiah gracefully walked a little further down the extensive hallway and turned into a small room.

The three Hebrews followed behind.

"You may speak freely," she invited, stopping to stand in the middle of the room.

"My Queen," Puah started. "This is Moses and his brother Aaron. They need an audience with Pharaoh."

"I am afraid that is impossible today." She folded her arms across her chest and tapped an elongated finger on her arm. "He is extremely busy with many important matters."

"I assure you, my Queen, this is an important matter as well."

She glanced into Puah's face. "Very well. I will try my best. Stay here." Queen Satiah gracefully walked away.

"Do you think this will work?" Aaron whispered.

"It has to." She kept her eyes on the hallway in which the Queen had disappeared.

It wasn't long before the woman was seen gliding back. "Follow me."

The three of them trailed the queen down the long maze of hallways. Each one more eloquently decorated than the last.

She watched Aaron's gaze inspect item after item as he witnessed Egyptian life at its finest. Paintings, furniture, room after room filled with anything a person could ask for. He probably had never been granted access to the palace before today.

Puah had walked the halls so many times, that the elegance had worn off many years ago.

She caught Moses out of the corner of her eye. His pace slowed behind the group. She imagined all of his childhood memories flooding back to his mind. This was not just the palace to him, it had been the home in which he'd grown up.

"Mighty Pharaoh," Queen Satiah announced as they approached the throne room.

Pharaoh Thutmose III sat upon a golden throne. It was decorated with regal symbols of Ra, the winged god he was believed to embody. He was robed in the best of linens and his gold and blue striped Nemes headdress sat perfectly atop his finest wig. He waved her forward.

"May I present Puah, Aaron, and Moses."

"Moses?" Pharaoh rose in such a quick motion that if Puah had blinked, she would have missed it. "Arrest him."

Guards rushed in like a mighty wind on either side of Moses and grabbed his arms.

"Wait." Puah stepped forward. "Hear them."

Pharaoh lifted his chin. "I do not have to listen to a midwife and I certainly do not have to agree to an audience with a murderer."

"We are here speaking on behalf of God," Aaron's voice rumbled through the vast space.

Pharaoh snorted. "If your precious Yahweh was so powerful, then why does he send slaves to speak to me?"

"The Lord God of Israel says, 'Let my people go, that they may hold a feast for me in the wilderness.' He has requested that we go three days journey into the desert to sacrifice unto Him."

"I know not your God." He lowered himself slowly. "Neither will I let Israel go."

Moses struggled against the guards.

Aaron stepped forward. "Our God has

requested-"

"I have heard enough about your god." He pounded his fist on the arm of his throne. "You are a lazy people. Lazy enough to have nothing better to do than bother me. Lazy enough to request leave to sacrifice to your god in the wilderness. Get out of here and go to work." He motioned to the guards with his chin. "I'll release you to return to the work for which you were born."

The guards dropped Moses' arms.

"Let it be known," Pharaoh Thutmose III's voice rang out. "For this disruption today, I will no longer provide straw for the Hebrews. They must collect their own straw for brick making, but must also maintain their quotas and not diminish by one brick." He sat back in his seat. "If they have time to go sacrifice to their god, then they have time to produce more structures for me."

The following morning, Puah walked through the palace hallways searching for Moses. She had already stopped by Aaron's home before the sun rose only to be told the two had headed back before Pharaoh.

When she passed the throne room, she heard voices and tipped her head inside.

Two men stood trembling in their short wraps and bare chests. They were Hebrew officers placed in charge of other slaves. Bruises covered their exposed skin and bandages were wrapped around their arms and legs.

"Why have you dealt with us so harshly?" one asked, his voice shook with fear. "The taskmasters request us to gather our own straw and then beat us for not providing the same number of bricks as in days past. We try to accomplish our duties, but they have taken away our straw. It is their fault we can't produce enough bricks."

"The fault lies with your own listless people," Pharaoh barked. "They have requested leave to make sacrifices to your god. No straw will be given to you, but you need to keep making the same number of bricks as before."

"Who has made such requests?" the other Hebrew official asked.

"Aaron and Moses." He lowered his gaze. "Now, get back to work."

The two rushed out of the room and into the hallway.

"Why would they do such a thing?" one of the men asked the other as they passed Puah.

"I don't know," the other said. "But we are going to find out."

She saw the figures of Moses and Aaron coming toward the two men.

"You!" the second officer yelled. He hurried to stand right in front of Moses. "What right do you have to speak for us?"

Aaron pushed his brother behind himself. "I beg your pardon, but you have no right to speak to us like that."

"We've just come from Pharaoh and he says that *this*." He pressed his bandaged arm in Aaron's face. "Is your fault."

"I'm sure I don't know anything-"

"You stirred his wrath," the other spoke.

"We are following God's orders."

The larger man took a step closer to place his body within inches of Aaron. "May the Lord judge you because you have turned us into a foul odor in the eyes of Pharaoh. With your request, you have given them all the excuse they need to slay us." He narrowed his eyes and then walked away.

With a shake of his head, the other followed.

"Don't worry about them," Aaron offered.

Moses huffed and stomped away.

Puah chased after him. Her old age slowed her steps, but she caught up to him. When she came to his side, she spoke softly, "Your brother is only trying to help."

He nodded roughly.

They walked at an unhurried pace through the hallway that led out of the palace.

"You know," she offered. "I could help with your speech."

Moses turned slightly to her.

"I've noticed you let Aaron do all the talking."

He nodded.

"I'm fluent in Egyptian because I treat both Hebrew and Egyptian women."

"Too long," he tried.

"You have been away a long time. But you were trained as an Egyptian, I'm sure you can learn quick enough."

He shrugged. "Aaron speaks."

"Aaron speaks well enough, but he's not you."

He looked at her with hesitation.

They stepped into the street and sunlight.

He sighed.

"Can I show you something? It'll take a few days journey, but I think it'll be worth it."

"Where?" he managed.

"Djeser-Djeseru in the valley of Deir el-Bahri. We can leave first thing in the morning."

He nodded slowly.

Puah didn't know if revealing the location early would make him change his mind. She wanted to be honest with him and allow him to hear her pleas. She just didn't know if he was ready to face what lay ahead.

Chapter 11

"And Pharaoh said, 'Who is the LORD, that I should obey his voice to let Israel go?' "
-EXODUS 5:2

Several days later, they entered the vast valley. When they came close to the temple, Puah slowed her steps. The heat blazed down on her leather skin. Her lungs took a few more breathes to get fresh air and her feet took a few more steps to keep up.

She hadn't visited this place in some time. She should have been worried about guards who would turn her away, but she knew there wouldn't be any. That was exactly why she had to bring Moses to this place.

Two rows of sphinxes, only slightly taller than a man, lined either side of the path. The once lush landscape was now dust. Those who were dispensed to keep the entrance well-groomed were reassigned or gone. She wandered around the open area for a few moments, taking it all in.

Then, she walked over to one of the many shriveled trees that stood in the small garden. She reached out to a withered leaf and gently rubbed it between her fingertips.

"The beautiful myrrh trees." She looked up at Moses, who had come to stand beside her. "A gift for you."

He looked around at the several bent over trees that dotted the area. Concern scrunched his face.

"There's more." She walked to the end of the garden and toward the significant incline. The main ramp led up to an open court area and then to another ramp that led into the temple. Each one held a set of stairs in the center, but the sides were flat.

Stone columns lined the faces of both levels. The many pillars made the front of the building appear as if it housed dozens of open doorways.

"I know this place," Moses' words faltered, but he tried to communicate with her in Egyptian.

"It's your mother's temple," she let the familiar second language flow over her tongue.

He cautiously took each step one at a time as if carrying the weight of a cornerstone on his shoulders.

Puah guided him into the main opening and matched his sluggish pace. Her eyes danced from wall to wall. It was hard to see anything without the torches lit, although the streams of sunlight coming in through the pillars helped.

"Hold on." She searched the walls until she found a torch. "There's got to be a flint around here somewhere." She felt around until her fingertips grazed a smooth stone. "Ah." Taking the rock, she struck the side of the wall while holding the top of the torch toward the flying sparks. She repeated the process until the oil-soaked cloth caught fire.

"I wanted you to see for yourself," she said, waving the light over the nearest wall. "He's destroying her legacy."

Moses faced the wall.

He placed his palm on the empty spot in the drawing. It had been hacked at with a sharp object until the relief was removed from its place.

He ran his fingers over the markings. "Why?"

"It's Pharaoh Thutmose III. He has become rather mad. His anger has been left to fester inside him like an infection all these years. It's blinded him." She rubbed the dent in the picture where Pharaoh Hatshepsu's image once lay. "This began slowly right after his son was born about ten years ago. He's trying to wipe her from the people's memory. It's only gotten increasingly worse recently."

"I didn't come to rule."

"If you could just speak with him…maybe…" Her eyes filled with tears. "Maybe you can get him to stop."

He sighed.

"I know she wasn't your birth mother, but she loved you dearly. You were her son. She pulled you from the Nile." The old midwife smiled up at him as her tears flowed out of her eyes and raced down her cheeks.

"She gave you everything as part of the royal family including granting you full rights as her firstborn son," her words rushed out. "She knew you were a Hebrew. I stood there that day as she held you in her arms and named you. She could have easily ordered you to be killed without so much as a backward glance. She had you trained in all Egyptian ways. She raised you from the time you were weaned until you…" Her voice trailed off.

"Left."

She nodded. "That must have been a difficult choice for you."

"No choice. Murder. Young. Prideful," his words spilled out in a mix of Hebrew and Egyptian. He shrugged and shook his head.

"You are no longer young," she tried in Hebrew. "And you are no longer running."

He nodded slowly but didn't meet her eyes.

She took him over to another wall. The mix of browns and greens depicted many boats. Sailors stood proudly carrying treasures from afar including many trees.

"Do you remember?" She pointed to the story.
He nodded. "Myrrh trees."

"For you. She asked them to bring back thirty-one. Your age at the time."

"Young."

"She loved you so." Puah moved the light to the part of the picture where Pharaoh Hatshepsu sat looking upon her returning voyagers.

The two took in each hieroglyphic along the many walls depicting Pharaoh Hatshepsu's rule.

"She brought peace to Egypt with a firm and loving hand."

He smiled wide. "Her house, too."

"You do remember." She grinned as she waved the light over more pictures. "She increased the mining of precious gems and increased trade with other lands."

They stopped at a particular part of one of the walls.

Moses searched the faces until he landed on another familiar one. "Senenmut."

She moved to see what he was looking at. The images were of Pharaoh Hatshepsu's most loyal aid, Senenmut.

"Friend," he said, placing his hand on the man's face.

"He became a trusted resource to her. They planned many projects throughout Egypt."

"Where?" He tapped the picture a few times.

"Pharaoh Thutmose III removed him from power before Hatshepsut was sealed in her sarcophagus. Not even the forty titles your mother bestowed upon him could save him from the new Pharaoh's wrath."

She walked a little further until she came upon a bust laying on the ground. Bending down, she picked it up and turned it over in her hands. It was an early depiction of the woman she missed dearly. She straightened and set it on a nearby stand.

Moses came and stood beside her.

They stared at the likeness together for a long moment.

Unlike most of the portrayals of the woman which filled her temple, this one was of her before she assumed the title of Pharaoh. Before her false beard and Nemes headdress. Queen Hatshepsut's feminine features were exquisitely enhanced in the limestone.

He picked it up and put his forehead to the statue's. He caressed her cheeks with his thumbs as tears fell from his eyes and onto the lifeless face staring back at him. "All...this...time..." he emphasized each word slowly as he pulled the bust slightly away from his face. "Almost forgot her face."

"She was a beautiful woman," she remarked.

He placed his finger on the chest of the bust and tapped it a few times. "Inside too."

"I remember when you left. She was so heartbroken." Puah rubbed the statue's head. "She missed you so much. She wanted all of this for you." She waved around the massive room. "Do you know she wouldn't let anyone touch her Senet game board?"

He kept his eyes on the face of the woman who had raised him.

"It sat just as it had in the middle of your game the day you left. I guess she always held out hope that you would return. It was to be you who brought peace to Egypt."

"Different calling."

"Moses?"

He looked up at her.

"Where did you go?"

"Midian. Rescued shepherdesses," his tongue faltered between the comfortable speech he learned in the wilderness and the brother language of his people. "Married oldest sister. Became family."

"But you came back?"

"Yahweh."

That was one word Puah knew. "God sent you back?"

"Mount Horeb," he struggled to explain. "Bush on fire, but not burned." He shrugged. "Got close. Heard God's voice say 'Go back. Pharaoh dead.' So, I come back." He returned his gaze to the statue in his hands. "Thought it was brother."

"You came back to rule?"

He shook his head. "Time to leave."

"I don't understand."

"God tell me He's going to free Hebrews."

"Why did you leave in the first place? You had royal protection. She could have pardoned you."

"Couldn't be Egyptian. Tried to be Hebrew. She might have pardoned, but still try to make me Pharaoh."

"I wish you had."

He scrunched his brow.

"If you had become Pharaoh, we could have been better. You would have had the power to change things. Pharaoh Thutmose III rules with harshness and pride."

"If I Pharaoh, things might change. But our people not free."

"How are you going to convince him to free us?"

"Not me. God."

"So?" she guessed. "Going back before Pharaoh?"

He nodded and returned the statue to its stand.

"Are you lazy slaves back again?" Pharaoh Thutmose III chuckled. "Do I need to increase your burden further?"

Puah stood with the two brothers in the throne room yet again. For weeks, she and Aaron had been working with Moses on his Egyptian. He had insisted on another audience with Pharaoh and she had been able to call on a favor with Queen Satiah. She feared it would be the last time.

Aaron stepped forward. "We speak for God-"

"Yes, yes. I have heard it before." Pharaoh adjusted himself on his throne to turn to his wife. "I am beginning to think this is some kind of mockery."

"God has requested that we go into the wilderness to sacrifice-"

"You come into my house." The royal man rose and balled his fists by his sides. "You demand that I release my slaves? You are fortunate that I do not throw all of you into prison. Guards!"

A set of soldiers maneuvered themselves between the group and Pharaoh, pressing them toward the doorway.

Aaron lifted his staff and threw it over their heads and onto the ground at Pharaoh's feet. As it hit the floor, the rod transformed into a serpent.

Queen Satiah gasped and held her hands over her open mouth.

"Merely a trick." He kicked the snake.

"It is no illusion," Aaron called, pushing back against the guard to ensure his voice was heard.

"Call for my magicians."

Within moments, Jannes and Jambres bowed before Pharaoh.

"May you live forever, Mighty Pharaoh," Jannes announced in his deep voice.

"This came from a rod." He pointed to the snake. "Can you do that?"

"It will be as you have spoken," Jambres agreed.

The two men performed a great dance of incantations and pleas to their gods. In one swift motion, they tossed two staffs down toward the decorated tile floor. Each transformed into serpents before everyone's eyes.

Queen Satiah moved her hands to her cheeks and then collapsed in a heap at her husband's feet.

Puah rushed to her side to fan her face.

"You see?" Pharaoh mocked. "Simply a trick."

Two of the Queen's maidens rushed into the room.

The queen stirred in Puah's arms. "S-s-snakes," she moaned.

"Get her back to her chamber." She helped them lift her to her feet. "I think she'll be well with some rest."

The women slowly aided the queen out of the room.

"Get these beasts out of my palace," Pharaoh ordered.

The guards stepped away from the group of Hebrews and scrambled after the three snakes.

Aaron's snake slithered swiftly toward the other two and consumed each in turn. Then it slipped through the grasp of each soldier leading them around the room.

"Catch that creature before he devours us all."

Aaron calmly walked over to his snake and picked it up. In his hand, the serpent straightened and transformed back into a rod. He looked right at Pharaoh. "Let our people go."

"Never." Pharaoh returned to his throne. With a quick nod, he signaled his guards.

Several brawny men shoved the group again toward the doorway.

As their feet slid further away, Puah twisted to Moses and pleaded with her eyes.

"Wait," Moses yelled in Egyptian.

Pharaoh raised his hand.

The warriors hesitated.

"I am the rightful heir to that throne you sit upon and you will hear me," Moses' words followed clear and strong like a vein of the Nile.

"You have no authority here," Pharaoh let disdain drip from each word.

"*You* have no authority over me." He struggled against the chest of the guard in front of him. "As first-born son of Pharaoh Hatshepsu, I demand you release me and pardon my transgression against Egypt."

"I do not have to agree to any of your demands and I should have you killed for speaking to me in such a way."

"Mighty Pharaoh," Queen Satiah's soft voice floated into the argument.

He turned in her direction.

She held her head and wobbled on her feet as she approached.

"Return to your chamber," he ordered.

"I must speak." She took another faltering step toward the group. "If you kill this Hebrew, their people could revolt. There are many of them and your warriors are spread far and wide protecting our borders. You do have the power to pardon him. If you do, perhaps their people will concede."

Pharaoh rubbed his beard. "I will grant your pardon on one condition. You leave this land and return to the dust of the wilderness from which you crawled."

"I can't do that."

"Then we have nothing left to discuss." He lifted his chin.

They were shoved from the room and escorted out of the palace.

"Now what?" Aaron asked, staring at the closed gate in front of them.

"Pray," Moses replied. He turned toward Puah. "God will do what He has said."

She watched the two brothers head in the direction of their home.

"God of the universe," she prayed aloud as she walked in the direction of her own house. "I wish you spoke to me like you do with Moses. I wish I could hear you as clear and bright so that my confidence in You might not shake like the sands under my feet. Give me strength to stand."

When she reached her house, Layla and Eliora stood outside waiting for her.

The young Hebrew woman rushed to embrace her.

As the mentor held her to arm's length, she noticed the fading light caught reflections in the girl's wet eyes. "What is it?"

Eliora wiped her face with the back of her hand. "I was so worried about you."

"I'm well. Nothing to fear." She embraced the woman once again and then made her way into the courtyard. "How did the day go for you two?"

"No, first you must tell us of your day," Eliora corrected as she handed her mentor a plate of fruit.

The Egyptian woman leaned upon a post.

Accepting the meal, Puah spoke plainly, "We went before Pharaoh again."

"And?"

"Nothing has changed except the level of Pharaoh's frustration with us."

"What else do you expect?" Layla asked.

"I don't fault him," the older woman said. "All of this is not my idea."

"But it's what God is calling Moses to do, right?" Eliora questioned.

Puah chewed the sweet bite in her mouth and swallowed. "That's what he says."

"I think that whole family is mad," Layla insisted. "And you too for being part of it."

"Don't speak to her like that," Eliora defended.

"She is entitled to her own opinion." Puah took another bite. "It all does sound quite mad."

"But it's what God wants." Eliora stomped her foot.

"Then He'll see to it," the mentor replied. She handed Eliora the empty plate. "Thank you. I think I shall get some rest now. It has been a long day."

The woman accepted the plate and nodded. "Of course."

"We shall speak more in the morning." She glanced over at Layla. "I think it best we all get some sleep."

The Egyptian woman closed her eyes and nodded slightly. "I think that's a good idea."

Each of her apprentices climbed the ladder to the upper room.

Puah took her well-worn straw mat and uncurled it on the floor in one of the smaller rooms. She pressed the edges down and laid upon it. Laying on her back, she looked to the ceiling and imagined the other two women sprawled out above her.

That night she dreamed of snakes and magicians. Of Moses and Aaron. Of the land promised to Abraham. Of the longing somewhere deep inside her to go and be free to be Hebrew. Of the overwhelming desire to stay and serve the women of Egypt.

Chapter 12

"Ye shall no more give the people straw to make brick, as heretofore: let them go and gather straw for themselves."
-EXODUS 5:7

Puah watched the pregnant woman take another lap around the small courtyard. She had been called to the home which lay on the fringes of the city of Pithom. Though the older midwife tried to stay close to her home city of Avaris in her advancing age, this couple reached out to her with their pleas for her expertise.

Nothing had given any indications of expecting issues during the few exams and check-ins she had performed over the last few months. But if there was one thing she always trusted, it was a woman's instincts.

"Do I have to keep walking?" Keziah panted. "I'm getting tired."

"I know, but it will help."

The woman's small feet shuffled in the sand to a slow pace. "My husband will be home soon."

Eliora looked to the open sky that was growing darker. "That means he'll be here to hold his baby."

"With any fortune," Layla added.

"Get some lamps ready," the mentor instructed her students. "I'm afraid this will be a long night."

The two rose from their place on the stone wall and entered the main room.

"There is some extra oil upstairs," Keziah called to them.

Eliora scampered up the ladder and returned with a few vessels.

"I remember when I could move that quickly." The pregnant woman rubbed her midsection. "Now, I feel like a river horse."

Puah chuckled. "You will once again leap around like a wild antelope." She stretched her aching back. "Unlike some of us whose time and stamina grow short."

"Greetings," a male voice called from the open gate. "I didn't know we were expecting guests."

"Husband." Keziah embraced the man. "These are the midwives I sent for. May I introduce Puah, Eliora, and Layla." She waved to the women. "This is my husband, Avram."

"Your wife has been a most gracious hostess," Eliora complimented.

"Am I to understand the reason for your visit is our child?"

"Yes," Puah agreed. "Your wife called for us a few hours ago when her pains began. I'm afraid she is progressing rather slow."

"I'm doing my best," the pregnant woman protested.

"It's not your fault," the midwife comforted. "It is common, especially with first births. The walking will help." She made a circle in the air with her finger.

"Guess I need to get back to it." The woman shrugged and walked the length of the open area again.

"Pardon me," Avram said. "I'm going to go wash up."

"There is some food in the kitchen if you're hungry," his wife called.

"Famished." He smiled a weary smile at her.

Puah watched the man walk to the washing bowl and use a rag to apply cool water to his skin. He wore a short skirt common to Egyptian men with nothing to cover his chest. His body was coated in dust mixed with sweat. As he washed the sand away, his dark olive complexion shone through. She could see long scars on his back that were in the latter stages of healing.

He stepped into another room and returned wearing a simple tunic more in line with what a Hebrew man would wear.

"Much better," he remarked as he sifted through the different bowls and plates collecting food into the bowl in his hand.

He sat on the wall next to Puah. "How long do you think?"

"Hard to tell."

He put a piece of yeast bread in his mouth.

"Do you work in the city?" Eliora asked, joining them on the wall.

He nodded while scooping up a pile of lentils. "I'm a brick maker."

"It must be hard work."

"It is. It's a lot harder now."

"Pharaoh's order," Eliora whispered.

"That's right. Before, we were provided with all the straw we needed. It was simply brought to us so we could work. Beautifully cut straw just lying in wait." He hung his head. "Now we have to gather it ourselves, but we're still expected to maintain our quota." He ate another bite before continuing, "I have to set out even earlier in the mornings, leaving Keziah here alone. We are new to the city. Had to move here when they relocated some us men closer to the quarries and she hasn't made many friends yet."

"She will." Layla grinned from the doorway.

"Then I have to rush through collecting my own straw before getting to work. It's gotten so bad lately that I've dug up the roots just to have enough provision for the bricks. Which means they are of lower quality, but Pharaoh doesn't seem to care about that."

"There is a lot Pharaoh doesn't seem to care about," Puah added.

"Ahh!" Keziah wailed.

Puah and Eliora jumped off the wall and ran to her side. Each grabbed an arm.

"That sounds like our signal," Eliora joked.

Avram hopped down and followed them inside. "What can I do?"

"Light the lamps for us."

He dropped his bowl on the kitchen table and set to work lighting the oil lamps Eliora had placed around the room.

"Easy," Puah said, helping the woman onto the birthing stones they had set upon their arrival. "I'm going to check you now."

She let out a bellow.

"You're doing well," Eliora encouraged.

"I can see the delay," Puah called from under them. "The baby is breech."

"W-W-What does that mean?" Keziah's words quivered.

"It means the baby is coming out backward. The baby was in the right position last week. Must have turned around again." She rocked back on her heels and rolled up her sleeves. "I'm not going to lie to you, this is going to hurt." She placed a hand on Keziah's thigh. "I'm going to have to stick my hands inside and try to turn the baby into position."

"What!"

"I know it sounds frightening, but I've done it before." She tucked back under her.

"Well?" the pregnant woman asked after several uncomfortable moments.

"Still trying." She was up to her wrists attempting to force the baby to turn around.

"Focus on me," Eliora offered. "Breathe like me." She steadied her breathing and locked gazes with the woman. "That's it."

Layla repositioned her arm. "You're doing well. Just keep breathing for us."

"This baby doesn't want to turn," Puah reported after some time. "Looks like he or she is going to be born backward." She snatched a clean linen from the pile and wiped some blood off her hands.

"But that can't work. I mean the head has to come first, right?"

"That's how we like it, but life doesn't always work out the way we want."

Keziah threw her head back into Eliora. "I can't do this. I'm not strong enough."

"Stop that right now," the student barked. "You listen to me. You are a Hebrew woman. You are strong and are capable of bringing this child into the world. Do you hear me?"

She bobbed her head slowly.

"Good. Now you're going to do everything Puah tells you to do and we are going to see your baby before this night is over."

"Ready?" the mentor asked.

Keziah sat up into position. "Ready."

Just before the first rays of sun lit the street, a new Hebrew girl lay in Puah's open arms. "She's here!"

Avram came near and kissed his wife's head. "I'm so proud of you."

"Is she well?"

"Very," Puah reported. "I'm just getting her cleaned up for you."

Keziah looked up to Eliora who was standing over her. "Thank you."

She smiled and shrugged.

"No, really. I couldn't have done it without you."

"I guess you were right, Momma," Layla commented.

Puah laid the new bundle on the woman's chest.

"About what?" Keziah tilted her head.

"You called for us even though we didn't believe there was anything wrong with your pregnancy."

She looked down at the suckling baby.

"There was little chance you could have delivered her on your own."

"You're right." She rubbed the baby's dark hair.

"Always trust your instincts," the older midwife said. "Always."

"What's her name?" Eliora asked.

She looked up to her husband and then back to her. "Liora. God's gift of light to me. And a thank you for helping me bring her into the world."

The woman blushed. "I'm honored."

Leaving instructions with the new mother and a promise to return in a few days, the midwives faced themselves toward home.

"You both did a great job," Puah said.

"Just doing my duty," Eliora commented.

"I love working with women," Layla added.

"You're both turning into fine midwives."

Eliora beamed.

As they walked along the way, a servant rushed toward them.

"Puah!" She shouted. "Come quickly!"

Upon recognizing the young girl, Puah picked up the hem of her dress and raced after her.

Being younger, Eliora and Layla quickly caught up and passed her.

When they made it to the end of the street, the servant pointed into a doorway and disappeared inside.

Puah saw her students follow and she pushed her aching muscles forward.

By the time she made it to the door, she could hear screams coming from within.

"I found Puah," the servant girl said. "She is here now."

"I'm here," Puah said, following the voices

deeper into the house. She found her apprentices already assisting a heavily pregnant Hebrew woman. "Hulda, you're not due for another few weeks, my dear."

The woman tried to smile, but it was torn away by the visibly strong pull of her midsection.

"Babies come when they want," the servant girl said. "You said that last time."

"So, I did," she remembered. "Well, let's have a look at you."

Layla and Eliora each supported Hulda's arms while she examined her patient.

"Well, today seems like a good day to have a baby, huh Hulda?" Puah asked.

"Ready?" the pregnant woman panted.

"Oh yes, very soon now."

"I'm glad I found you," the servant said with relief.

"Yahweh has been good to you, Hulda. I was just coming from visiting a new patient. Dara happened to catch us in town. I don't often come out this far. This baby would be here before any midwife could have been."

Hulda let out a yelp and then a shout.

"Okay ladies, I say it's about time to meet this little one."

After less than an hour of pushing, Hulda welcomed a strong son into the world.

"Look at him," Puah said, holding the squirming baby up to show his mother. "He's handsome."

Eliora wiped away some sweat from the new mother's brow. "He is very handsome."

"He looks like his father." She grinned.

"Then he will be one happy man," Layla teased.

Eliora cleaned the newborn and wrapped him in a fresh set of linens before handing him to his mother. "There you are."

"Thank you." Hulda nuzzled her boy.

"You know," Layla said, watching the boy drink. "There is another young mother who gave birth today, Keziah."

"I think I met her in the market a few months ago."

"They are new to town and don't have many friends."

"Say no more." The woman smiled a knowing little smile. "I'll be sure to make them feel welcome."

"Wonderful. I was hoping you would."

"I'll be by to check on you in a few days," Puah promised as they departed.

"Another healthy baby," Eliora remarked when they were back on the street.

"Yes." Puah nodded. "Layla, that was a very kind act to help those women get connected."

"I know how it feels to be left out." She shrugged. "Their children will be the same age. Hulda has an older child so she can help answer any questions Keziah may have. They can support each other. It just made sense."

"It was a brilliant idea. Why don't you head home and start some food? Eliora and I can get these linens washed up before we head back."

"My pleasure," the girl agreed and headed home.

The other two made their way toward the large Nile River.

Once they reached the banks, each lifted the back of their skirt up between their legs and tucked them into their belt so they could wade into the shallows.

"The frigid water feels so good," Eliora said, wiggling her bare toes into the silty mud.

Puah took out a blood-soaked rag from her bag and dipped it into the river. "Sure does." She rang out the cloth.

The younger woman mimicked her movements with another cloth.

Puah dipped the linen back into the water and twisted the rag. "Odd."

Her student looked over at her. "What?"

She dipped the cloth back into the water, lifted it out, and twisted.

Eliora watched the water flow red from the rag. "We did just use them to clean a newborn."

"I know that," Puah shot her apprentice a superior glance. "But look." She pointed toward the water that was shifting from clear to a deep crimson.

"There couldn't have been that much blood in these rags."

"The river is changing colors all around us." She motioned to the water. "Not just where we're rinsing out the linens."

"What could this mean?"

Puah shook her head. "I'm not sure." She reached her hand into the water and lifted it. Rubbing her fingers together, she studied the sticky, thick liquid. "Blood?"

In the same moment, splashing started all around them.

"What is that?" Eliora said, wading back toward the bank of the river.

"Look." Puah pointed.

She followed her gaze to the shore.

Dozens of fish jumped onto the banks to escape the bloody water.

"They'll die if they stay on land," Eliora said.

"They'll die if they stay in the blood," she responded as she made it to the shore. "Come, let us go see Neith. Maybe we can discover the truth."

"The magician's wife?"

"Yes. I should be able to speak with her."

The two women soon found themselves standing in Pharaoh's palace describing what they had witnessed to Neith.

"It could have been algae," the older woman suggested. "It's happened before."

"That wasn't algae. It was blood," Puah stated simply. "I know blood. I'm a midwife."

"I don't know what Moses did to the waters, but Khnum will set it right. He wouldn't let some Hebrew slave disgrace the Nile."

Puah wanted to argue, but she barely understood what was happening.

"Besides," Neith continued. "Jannes and Jambres have already duplicated the trick."

"What?"

"Yes." The woman who was letting her boredom for the whole thing be heard in her voice. "Moses was in here yesterday with his brother."

"Moses?" Eliora whispered.

"They came to Pharaoh requesting to be seen and demanding he let all the Hebrew people leave Egypt. Can you imagine the boldness of such a man? Pharaoh should have had him killed on the spot."

"Why didn't he?" the student asked.

"I see you haven't revealed much to your young apprentice."

Puah turned to Eliora. "A very long time ago, my mentor, Shiphrah, and I were brought before Pharaoh. He ordered us to kill all Hebrew boys born under our care."

"But you didn't. You helped save many a Hebrew baby boy. You've told me the story."

"Not all of it," Neith interjected.

"We did help rescue several children. One of them was Moses. He was such a beautiful child. How I imagine an angel must look. Strong and radiant."

"And?"

"His parents hid him for three months. I begged them to let me take him away to a safer place, but they wouldn't have it. They insisted they could look out for him."

"What happened after three months?"

"His mother got this ridiculous idea."

"What?"

"She made a basket, placed Moses in it, and put it in the Nile."

"She did what?" The young woman put her hands on her flushed cheeks.

"I know. I couldn't believe it. The one place we were trying to keep babies out of, she willingly put him in."

"But if she did, then how can he be the same Moses?"

"His sister, Miriam, followed the basket down the river. She watched as it floated near where Pharaoh's daughter was bathing. When the princess discovered the baby inside, she decided to keep him and raise him as her own."

"That's quite a story."

"That's only part of it. Miriam was brave enough to tell the princess she could find a Hebrew woman to nurse the child for her. Guess who she went to fetch?"

"Her mother?" Eliora smiled.

The mentor nodded. "Jochebed got to raise her son all while being paid to do so. Once Moses was weaned, she returned him to the princess and he was raised as a son of Pharaoh."

"I still don't understand."

"Don't you see?" Neith moaned. "Moses has been gone for forty years. The Pharaoh he has been standing before is his brother. The two were raised together."

"Pharaoh couldn't kill his own brother then?" the younger woman wondered.

"I don't think it was so much family loyalty as fear of revolution," the older midwife interjected.

"How do you know?" Eliora asked.

"She was there," Neith revealed.

"Queen Satiah cautioned her husband about our numbers against his outstretched army. I'm sure Pharaoh has rectified that situation by now. I saw Aaron's rod turn into a snake and devour the rods of the magicians which they had transformed into snakes. You said Jannes copied the blood as well?"

Neith nodded. "I watched the two of them turn a bowl of water to blood with my own two eyes."

"But not the entire Nile," Eliora whispered under her breath.

The magician's wife glared at her. "A trick is a

trick, no matter the scale," she stated, clearly unamused.

The two women excused themselves and headed home.

"I can't believe you never told me that story," Eliora commented.

"I've tried to hide it." Puah sighed. "What I did, what we did, was disobedience."

"To a madman."

"That is true, but it still could have meant death for me and for all the ones helping us."

"So, you know Moses well?"

The older midwife nodded slightly. "I was there for his birth, I was there when Princess Hatshepsut named him, and I watched him grow up in the palace."

"That's why you've gone to see him so much since his return."

Puah paused.

"Does he listen to your council?" Eliora asked.

"Some." She started walking again. "I went the first time because I needed to show him what Pharaoh was doing. I needed to make him see."

"Do you think it's true what Neith said that it was Moses who turned the Nile to blood?"

She shrugged her tired shoulders. "I'm not sure."

"Do you think you'll visit him again?" The young girl brightened.

"I have a feeling we are all going to be seeing

more of Moses. He said it's God's plan for us to leave Egypt."

"Can I come next time?"

She wrapped her arm around the younger woman's waist. "Sure. You'll love Miriam. You remind me a lot of her."

Chapter 13

"And all the Egyptians digged round about the river for water to drink; for they could not drink of the water of the river."
-EXODUS 7:24

"It's been seven days," Eliora said to Puah as they dug by the river for freshwater. "When will this end?"

The older woman held her nose as the winds shifted. The scent of blood had never bothered her before, but when it filled an entire river and then was heated by the scorching sun, it made her stomach turn. "I don't know. My hope is soon. It's taking far too long to collect freshwater this way."

"We have several-"

She straightened to see her apprentice's' mouth hanging open. "What is it?"

The girl pointed to the Nile.

Puah looked over her shoulder just in time to see an army of frogs crawling out of the water and heading straight for them.

Both women fled.

"I've never seen so many frogs in all my life," the younger woman called over her shoulder.

"Neither have I."

The two found refuge in their home, but it was only for a short time. As the day went on, the frogs increased in number to the point they could crawl into the high windows.

They spent the next two days hunched over with hand brooms wrangling frogs from every inch of the house until they were too tired to fight anymore.

"Let them hop," Puah said as she dropped onto a pile of pillows with her broom still in her hand. "There are just too many of them."

A knock came at their gate.

"Would you get that?" she asked. "I don't think these old bones could stand right now."

Eliora nodded and answered the door.

A few moments later, Neith stood looking down on Puah. "You lounge around while our cities are overrun with frogs?"

As she spoke, several frogs hopped between the women.

The old midwife tightened her grip on the broom handle. She hadn't decided if she'd aim for the nearest frog or her guest. "Neith, I'm too tired to-"

"Tell that Moses of yours to get rid of these stupid frogs," the woman interrupted and kicked a frog across the room that had hopped onto her foot.

"Moses?" she straightened at his name.

"Yes. Him again. He told Pharaoh that if he didn't let your people go, he'd bring a plague of frogs on our land."

"Did your husband duplicate this trick too?" Eliora asked, sweeping away another group of frogs.

"As a matter of fact, he did." She placed her hands on her ample hips.

"Great." The girl rolled her eyes. "Now we have twice as many frogs."

"He was just showing Moses that we Egyptians have power too." Neith crossed her arms over her chest and squared her shoulders.

"Power? How about you ask that husband of yours to reverse these tricks instead of just copying them. That'd be some real power."

"Puah, are you going to let your apprentice speak to me in such a disrespectful manner?"

"Peace, Eliora."

"May the Goddess Heqt curse you."

"Frog lady?" the student chuckled. "Tell her to come get her kids."

"They are only leaving the river because Moses turned it to blood." She waved toward the direction of the Nile. "Where do you expect them to go? Once the river is clean again, they'll go back."

Puah rubbed her temples. "What is all this madness?" she asked herself while the other two women continued to quarrel.

"Besides, Pharaoh already demanded Moses clean up his messes." The magician's wife kicked another frog to emphasize her point.

"And how's that?" Eliora removed a frog which had jumped onto her head.

"Moses and Aaron prayed to your God and they said the frogs will be gone tomorrow. Hopefully, the Nile will soon be back to normal as well."

"Anything else?" Puah asked, letting her exhaustion seep into her words and hoping her friend would receive the underlying message loud and clear.

"Yes, tell Moses to stop these games." Neith turned to leave, but not before stomping on a few poor creatures on her way out.

The midwife let out a long sigh and looked at the ceiling.

"Do you think she's right?" Eliora said, holding a giant frog in her hand and examining it.

"About what?"

"Moses?"

Puah looked at her. "What do you mean?"

"Do you think he'd listen to you?"

"I'm no one important."

"You helped spare his life. Surely he'd listen if you spoke."

She sighed. "It couldn't hurt to try." She closed her eyes. "We'll go see him in the morning."

The next morning, Puah awoke to a great stench. "What is that smell?" she asked, searching the house.

"The frogs are baking in this heat," Eliora answered. She was already working on sweeping the dead bodies out of the house with a scarf wrapped around her face to help with the smell. "Everyone else is doing the same." She nodded toward the open gate in the courtyard.

The older woman stepped into the bright morning sun to see piles of dead frogs lining the street in both directions. "That's not going to be good for the land."

"Tell me about it," the apprentice said as she swept another heap out the gate and onto the pile in front of their house.

"Where's Layla?"

"She rose early too. Said sweeping frogs wasn't part of her duties and headed out to make some rounds."

Puah rubbed her temples. The pressure didn't help to work out the headache that had not left her since the previous day.

"Want me to get you some breakfast?" the younger girl offered as she dumped another pile of dead bodies onto the stack she had started outside their gate.

"I don't think if even you could lay out the finest food in all of Egypt from Pharaoh's own table could I eat a bite right now." She sighed.

"Do you want to make some visits?"

"A visit, yes, but not to one of our patients."

"Where to?" She grabbed a supply bag.

"I think it's time we visit Moses."

Eliora snatched some bread and dried fruit and shoved them into her bag. "Ready."

When they entered Aaron's home, Puah introduced her young apprentice to the group of siblings.

"You are favored to learn from such a woman," Miriam commented.

"She is very knowledgeable about our craft. Under her, our guild has prospered."

"We have something to discuss besides me," Puah added. "What is the purpose behind these displays?"

"River to blood? Frogs?" Eliora recounted.

"To demonstrate to Pharaoh that our God is the true God of this world," Moses acknowledged. "Pharaoh refuses to let our people go. He has hardened his heart."

"And you think plaguing him will change his mind?" the apprentice asked.

"It's not my idea, young one." Moses went to the courtyard gate. "I see the frogs are clearing." He motioned to the piles with his chin.

"They have no longer increased," Eliora

answered. "But we are going to be cleaning up their bodies for a while."

Moses sighed. "This is not the end I'm afraid. It is merely the beginning. God has already instructed me in the next plague."

"Another one!" Eliora shouted.

"Peace," Puah chided.

"Let her speak. I'm just as much angered. Not with God for bringing these plagues, but with my brother for closing off his heart to God. If only he would listen, we wouldn't have to go through this."

"What's next?"

Moses stepped over to Aaron, who had stayed inside the main room. "Show them."

The older brother walked into the open courtyard. He stretched his rod across the sand and then smacked the dust with the stick.

Puah and Eliora's eyes were fixed on the cloud of dust as it rose in the air and then settled back to the ground.

"I don't-" the older midwife began, but a scream from Eliora interrupted her.

"Lice!" The girl scrambled away and stood on the other side of the gate peering in.

"Lice?" the midwife asked.

"I don't pick them." Moses shrugged. "I just perform them."

The next morning, Puah's gate opened wide without a knock to precede it.

"Lice?" Neith asked, itching her scalp as she stood in the courtyard. "Why did it have to be lice?"

"I don't know," Puah answered while she scratched her own head.

"There are lice in my favorite wig." She shook the limp bundle of hair at her friend. "I thought you were supposed to speak with Moses about stopping these plagues. Not increasing them."

"I did, but he said this is all God's doing not his."

"Doesn't your God listen to the cries of his people?"

"Doesn't your Pharaoh listen to reason?" Eliora interjected as she stepped into the courtyard.

"I've had my fill of you."

"I've had my fill of all of it."

"Peace, ladies," the mentor requested. "It doesn't do any good to turn on one another."

"Where are those frogs when we need them?" Eliora asked.

"You joke even now?" Neith fumed. "Geb is punishing your smart mouth."

"Your god of dust certainly has a sense of humor."

"My husband thinks this is the finger of your God."

"I agree," Puah said.

"I wish Pharaoh did too," Eliora added.

Chapter 14

"…and the houses of the Egyptians shall be full of swarms of flies, and also the ground whereon they are."
-EXODUS 8:21

A few months later as the season changed into the cooler month of Kislev, Puah and Eliora visited the pregnant Sofh in Memphis.

"Have you come to torment me like your leader?"

"We have come to check on your progress." Puah ignored the jab.

"Goddess Khepri will deal harshly with all of you for this torture." She batted away a group of flies from the most recent plague that had collected around her face.

"She can move the sun, but she can't get rid of the flies?" Eliora said.

"Those rotting piles of frog corpses are attracting more and more bugs," Sofh scolded. "First the lice and now these annoying flies."

"It's been months. The frogs have long been

turned to dust. Besides," Eliora corrected. "They only seem to be bothering the Egyptians. We don't have any flies in the land of Goshen."

Sofh swatted away another group of flies. "Ugh! Get them out of here."

Aria scurried in with a large palm frond to whack away the pests.

"Let's focus on our visit," Puah suggested. "How are you doing?"

"Other than the flies that buzz in my ears and fill my beautiful home night and day?"

"Yes."

"Miserable."

"The liquids are not helping?"

"Somewhat, but I have to sip on the stuff throughout the day."

"I see." She thought a moment. "Are you eating enough?"

Sofh huffed. "Nothing tastes good anymore."

"I understand, but you must eat for the baby. Eliora and I can leave some ideas for Aria to try. Maybe we can find some new dishes that you'll enjoy."

"I will try."

"Good." Puah retrieved her bag. "We shall look in on you again on another day."

"Where to next?" Eliora said as they entered the street.

"I'm going to go see Moses. You're welcome to join me."

Puah and her student were greeted with open arms into Aaron's home. The small building housed all three siblings and both men's families. Still, they warmly opened their space to the two midwives.

"Moses and Aaron are upstairs," Elisheba said. "I'll fetch them for you."

She climbed up the ladder and returned with her husband and brother-in-law.

"Greetings," they said.

"And to you." Puah bowed. "I'm seeking report of your recent audience with Pharaoh."

"How do you always know?" Aaron asked.

She shrugged. "Tell a woman, tell the world."

Moses chuckled.

"That's the truth," Miriam called from the kitchen. "I'll have some bowls of stew ready soon. Sit and chat."

The two midwives made themselves comfortable on pillows in the main room.

"So?" Puah prodded.

"Pharaoh said we could go make our sacrifices."

"That's wonderful news," Eliora boasted.

"He said we could only go a short distance away and the men can go alone," Moses explained.

"Oh." The young apprentice hung her head.

"What else did he say?" Puah asked.

"He asked me to pray for him."

"He sure needs that," Eliora snapped.

"He simply wants me to ask God to remove the swarms." Moses clarified as he sat.

"Are you?" Eliora questioned.

Moses sighed. "Yes."

"You know he'll just recant again like the previous times." The older midwife criticized.

"I know, but just because someone else doesn't keep their word doesn't mean I shouldn't keep mine." He stepped into the open courtyard and prayed aloud, "Lord God of the universe, hear your servant's plea. Remove the swarms of flies from Pharaoh, from his servants, and from his people."

After a warm meal together, Moses and Aaron readied themselves to meet the elders in the city. They had placed on their outer coats and grabbed their rods.

"Moses," a strange voice rumbled from the other side of the gate.

Aaron looked to Miriam, who shrugged.

The younger brother went to the gate and opened it.

"Moses?" A royal guard stood towering over him.

"Yes?"

"I have a message from Pharaoh." He puffed out his chest. "He has withdrawn his permission for you to leave Goshen. You and your people are not permitted to go into the wilderness."

"I understand." He shut the gate and faced the

group.

"Moses." Miriam took a step toward him. "I'm so sorry-"

He held up his hand. "I'm going to go pray some more." He crawled up the ladder and disappeared into the upper room.

Miriam spread her palms toward the midwives.

"We'll see ourselves out," Puah offered with a hug. "He just needs some time."

The next day, Puah woke to a bright sun pouring into the room from the doorway to the courtyard. She washed and readied herself for the day.

"Is Layla gone again?" she asked, entering the kitchen.

Eliora had prepared a large spread and was cleaning the final few dishes. "Yes." She paused for a moment. "She grows more and more distant with each passing day."

The mentor came to stand next to her. She placed a reassuring hand on her shoulder. "I'll speak with her."

The younger girl smiled. "Thanks." She dried the dish in her hand and put it away. "Ready to head into Peru-nefer?"

Puah grabbed the outstretched bag from her apprentice. "I guess we shall see."

"What do you think we'll find?" Eliora wondered. "Maybe another plague is waiting for us?"

"I don't know."

They made their way through the busy streets and south into the royal city.

"I don't see any flies."

"I guess Moses' prayer worked."

At the first Egyptian house, Puah cautiously knocked on the door.

A sheepish woman edged the gate open. "Yes?"

"Greetings, Tira," Puah said. "We're here to see Ouei."

"Oh, yes." The Hebrew servant widened the entrance. "Please, come in. She's in the garden."

The two midwives walked through the main hallway and out into the back portion of the property. They found their patient pulling weeds.

"Greetings," Puah called.

"Welcome." The woman straightened and came to them. "Isn't it a beautiful day?"

"It is," the older midwife agreed.

"Especially without all those flies." She tossed a handful of weeds into a nearby pile. "I can finally get out here and enjoy the sunrays Ra has given us." She lifted her face toward the clear day above them.

"Would you mind if we interrupt you for a short time to check on your progress."

She sighed. "I supposed I can go inside for a few moments."

"Wonderful." Puah turned toward the house.

"Let's have a look at you."

As the women prepared a place inside and made the pregnant woman comfortable, a servant came running in.

"Begging your deepest pardon." He bowed so low, he almost hit the floor. "But there is something wrong."

Ouei looked at the two women.

Puah shrugged. "We can wait."

They assisted her off the couch and followed behind the servant.

He rushed toward the cattle yards at the back corner of the property.

The three women came close to the open gate.

"What seems to be the problem?" Ouei asked her group of servants.

One stood. "We thought maybe she was in labor. That's why we sent Jahi to fetch you."

"And?"

"They all seem to be sick." He pointed to the four cows laying at his feet.

"When will my husband return?"

"He said before nightfall, but I don't think they can wait."

"Can you look at them?" Ouei asked Puah.

"I don't think I could help. I take care of babies, not cattle."

"Please?"

She sighed. "I'll try." Stepping into the straw-lined area, she knelt next to one of the cows.

The animal bellowed low.

"Easy girl," she whispered.

"Well?"

"She certainly seems ill. I think you should call for help from someone who knows more about these matters."

Ouei nodded. "I believe you're right. I'll send word at once."

"Maybe we should check on you another day," Eliora offered.

"I think that's best."

"We can see ourselves out."

Puah shut the main gate behind them but held her hand on the door.

"What is it?" her student inquired.

"Do you think…"

"It's possible."

She traced the grain of the wood with her fingertip. "We're close to the palace. Let's go see Neith."

They quickly found their friend inside the majestic walls of the palace complex.

"I see you've received the news as well," Neith said as they sat on one of the comfortable couches in the woman's private chamber.

"News?" Puah asked.

"The next plague your Moses has issued on Egypt."

Eliora exchanged a glance with her mentor.

"A plague of sickness on our cattle, horses,

donkeys, camels, oxen, and even down to our sheep."

"We've seen it."

Neith paced around the room and twisted the sash at her side. "We've done something to upset Hathor."

"You've done something to upset Yahweh," Eliora retorted.

"Those pests your God has cast upon us transported disease with their bites."

Eliora stood. "Your gods-"

"I think that's quite enough." Puah rose between the two of them. "We shall excuse ourselves."

"I think that's best."

The midwives left the room and headed down a side hallway.

"These Egyptians are never going to get it." Eliora shook her head as they walked. "I'm starting to believe none of these plagues are a coincidence."

"What do you mean?"

"The Nile, the frogs, the lice, and the flies." She counted each on her fingers. "Now the cattle. Each is a representation of one of their major deities."

"You're right Khnum and Hapi, Heqt, Geb, Khepri, and now Hathor. Each of them being brought down by the power of our God."

A figure caught Puah's attention out of the

corner of her eye. She moved to see the person who was rushing toward a nearby hallway.

"Moses?" She hurried after him.

Eliora kept up with her.

When they reached him, he twisted to face them.

"His heart is so hard," Moses lamented.

"Pharaoh?"

He nodded.

"He's never going to let us go, is he?" Eliora asked.

"No." He hung his head and turned away.

Puah watched his slumped figure disappear into the shadows.

The women left the palace, heading north toward their home.

"I wish there were more to do to help," Eliora offered.

"Me too."

They walked in silence until they reached Avaris' city limits.

"Go on ahead," the mentor said.

"Are you sure?"

"Yes. I'm well. I just need a few moments to pray."

"I'll see you inside." The younger woman picked up her pace and turned the corner toward their home.

"God," Puah prayed aloud. "I understand all of this is your way of revealing yourself to the

Egyptians. Have mercy on us. Have mercy on them."

"Puah!" a high voice called from over a short stone wall.

She turned to see a large woman waving her over. "Greetings, Yael." She adjusted her footsteps toward the woman and leaned on the half wall.

"Can I offer you a cup of water?" She held out a small cup.

"I'm actually on my way home now." She pointed in the direction she was heading.

"Oh please?" The women opened her gate and entered the street. "I would love some company."

Puah smiled. "I supposed a few moments."

"Wonderful." The woman linked her arm in Puah's and led her into the courtyard.

"How are you?" she asked as she accepted the cup and sat on the stone wall.

"Feeling much better." She rubbed her belly.

"That's good to hear."

"I heard about the Egyptian cattle."

The old midwife scarcely had the energy to nod.

"I was so afraid for our stock."

The midwife's attention sharpened. "Yours?"

"Yes." She lifted a cup to her own lips. "As soon as I heard, I rushed to the stable to check on our cattle."

"And?"

"They are all well."

"Thank God."

"Indeed."

She took a sip from the cup in her hand. The cool liquid quenched the thirst she had ignored all day. "Thank you."

"My pleasure."

She looked at the woman's rounded stomach. "Not much longer."

The woman beamed. "I can't wait."

"Well, if you'll excuse me." She rose and handed her the cup. "I need to get home."

"Stop by anytime. My gate is always open to you."

She smiled a weary smile. "That means a lot."

When the gate shut behind her, Puah's feet took her home with a little more lightness. Her heart was still heavy for the Egyptians, but it was nice to confirm her people weren't suffering under these plagues. God was truly merciful toward His people.

Chapter 15

"And the magicians could not stand before Moses because of the boils; for the boil was upon the magicians, and upon all the Egyptians."
-EXODUS 9:11

1446 B.C.

Eliora and Puah easily maneuvered the streets of Memphis on foot.

"I spoke with Layla," the mentor said as they walked.

"And?" the younger woman's eyebrows rose with anticipation.

She sighed. "She is getting a lot of pressure from her family to separate herself from us."

"That's ridiculous."

"That's reality."

"So, she is giving up being your apprentice?"

"She is going to take some time and work with the Egyptian midwives in the south."

Eliora opened her mouth to speak.

"For now," Puah added before her student could say a word. "We'll see if things change."

"Do you think this new month will bring change?" the younger woman asked.

"I've been praying for such," she noted as they came to the gate of the home where they had been increasingly requested.

"I'm glad to see you." Aria welcomed them in with haste. "Mistress has been calling for you all day."

"We have become much busier these days," Puah agreed.

"Silence all the unnecessary chatter and tend to me," Sofh called from the master bedroom just off to the right of the main hallway.

"Of course," Puah said as they rounded the corner to find her still lying in bed. "Can you tell me what's troubling you?"

"Your deity is troubling me," she whined. "Look at my beautiful skin." She lifted the sleeves of her white robe to reveal large boils covering her once flawless complexion. "Just look at all that."

The old midwife walked to the bed and leaned over to examine the woman's arms carefully. "I see. Are they painful?"

"Incredibly. I'd almost rather have the flies back."

"I can take care of those if you wish, but it's not a painless procedure."

"Anything will be better than this. I haven't

been able to sleep." She lifted her arm to her face as if shielding it from the sun. "I've sacrificed night and day to Isis, but she hasn't heard my pleas."

"Maybe she's asleep," Eliora murmured to herself behind Puah.

"I also have to warn you that the relief could leave behind some scarring," she revealed hoping to cover Eliora's voice.

"Is there anything else you can do instead?"

"Unfortunately, no. We need to drain them to release the buildup. You can get very sick otherwise."

"If you must." Sofh flipped her head to the side.

"How are you besides the boils? Baby moving well?" Puah brought her bag to the nearby table and unpacked the tools she would need.

"Yes, he moves all the time."

"A boy?" Eliora chimed.

"What else would I have?" Sofh rolled her eyes.

"A girl?" Eliora whispered to the rhetorical question. She stepped to her mentor's side to assist her.

"Watch your words, my young one," Puah instructed in her ear in Hebrew.

"Please give me something to do before I say any more," she replied back in the same tongue.

"Work on getting the bandages laid out while I ready a place."

Eliora took over the tools as Puah headed back to the bedside.

"Now, I'm going to put some fresh linens down around you so we can contain the mess."

"Mess?" Sofh raised both eyebrows.

"I warned you. This is not going to be pleasant."

"Aria?" Puah beckoned.

"Yes?" The Hebrew servant came to the doorway.

"Would you draw us some fresh water from the well and mix it with wine. I'm going to need to clean those infected areas."

She bowed and was back swiftly with two large bowls just as Puah was finished preparing the area.

"Ready?" the midwife asked as she held up a sharp knife.

"What are you going to do with that?"

"I have to open the boils to let the infection drain out."

"Will this harm my baby?"

"No. You are in very capable hands." Puah put a knee on the bed next to Sofh and lanced the first boil on her outstretched arm.

"Ouch!" She recoiled. "Are all of them going to hurt like that?"

"I'm afraid so." The midwife held her palm out. "I need to keep going. It'll be best if you allow me to continue working so Eliora can bandage the areas as soon as I finish."

The young student stood by with a freshly anointed bandage in her hand.

Puah cut into another sore.

Sofh winced.

Eliora reached over to dab her arm with a cloth dripping with the water and wine mixture before applying the first covering.

"How come none of you have any boils?" Sofh seethed through gritted teeth.

"Only by God's grace," Eliora answered.

"Ha," The woman growled. "Gods don't offer grace. They only seek appeasement."

"Ours offers it," the apprentice said as she turned to reach for another bandage.

Several hours later, Eliora wrapped the last bandage. "All done."

"Aria, fetch my looking glass."

The servant nodded and hurried to complete her task. Upon returning, she held up the polished brass to her mistress.

"I look wretched."

"Better than boils," Eliora said before placing her hand over her mouth and excusing herself with a tray of dirty linens before her mentor could do it for her.

Sofh adjusted the oval again and again to see different angles of herself. "I look like a mummified body."

"At least the pain will lessen now," Puah said. "You should be able to get some rest."

"At least there is that." She put the brass beside her on the bed.

"It won't be much longer now before you meet your baby." Puah fixed one of her pillows to make her more comfortable and set to work repacking her medical bag.

"I just pray Imhotep heals me of this wretchedness before my baby sees me. What will he think of a mummified mother?"

Eliora tried to stifle a chuckle as she entered the room at the same time the question was asked, but she was unsuccessful. Much to the dismay of Sofh and Puah.

"You find this all very funny, do you?" the pregnant woman asked.

She straightened. "No, mistress. Forgive me."

"That will be all. You can see yourselves out."

"As you wish." Puah tossed her bag over her shoulder, bowed, and pushed her student into the hallway. "Rest well," she called to her patient. "Send for us if you have need of anything before the baby comes."

"I, for one, can't wait until she has that baby," Eliora breathed as they stepped into the cool air.

"Oh, you do?"

"Yes, so she'll stop calling on us."

"A woman in need is a woman in need. It doesn't matter how she treats us."

"I know. But would it kill her to treat us with a little respect? I mean, we do take care of her after all."

Puah nodded.

"I have half a mind to mix up a lotion to turn her skin green."

"You wouldn't!"

"No." She giggled. "But it's fun to think about."

"I do beg of you, young one, that you learn to hold your tongue in the presence of our patients. Just because a thought crosses your mind doesn't mean it needs to cross your lips."

"Forgive me." She lowered her gaze. "Sometimes I just can't help myself."

"Restraint comes with age," she offered. "You'll get better."

"Then you must have the restraint of the Nile," the girl teased.

Puah swatted at her with her medical bag. "That's quite enough from your lips for one day."

Eliora smiled and rushed ahead to walk backward. "You know…we're close to Aaron's place."

The mentor raised an eyebrow. "And?"

"I'm getting hungry." She rubbed her slender stomach. "Do you think they would mind if we stopped by for a mid-day meal?"

"Well…"

"Please?" the younger girl folded her hands and pleaded.

"I supposed."

"Wonderful." She turned back to face the right direction and slowed to match her mentor's pace.

Miriam greeted the two women before they completely made it into the courtyard. "I was praying for you this very morning."

"You were?" Puah asked as she put her bag near the front gate.

"I was asking God to bless the work of your hands since I know they have been incredibly busy as of late."

"You speak much truth," the older midwife agreed. She sat on the short stone wall and stretched her legs.

"Something smells delightful." Eliora sniffed the air.

"Where are my manners?" Miriam ducked into the kitchen. "Let me get you some bowls."

"Where are your brothers?" Puah called to her.

"They went into the city again."

"To see Pharaoh?" Eliora asked.

Miriam shrugged. "Who else?"

"Do you expect them back soon?"

"I-"

"How many more times are we going to do this?" Aaron's gruff voice entered the courtyard before he did. "Honestly, brother. Do you believe Pharaoh will ever change his mind?"

"God will keep His promises regardless of Pharaoh's actions."

The two men closed the gate behind them and entered the courtyard without acknowledging anyone there.

"Then why do we constantly put ourselves in front of him?" the older brother asked.

"This is what God has instructed me to do."

Aaron huffed and climbed the ladder in silence.

"Miriam tells us you've been to see Pharaoh again," Puah stated.

Moses watched his brother's form disappear. "Yes, early this morning."

"And?" Eliora wondered.

"And," Moses took a seat on the wall, "he refuses once again to let our people go."

"I don't see how he can harden his heart so against such great powers," Miriam said, handing him a bowl of lentils.

"Even his own magicians could not stand before us today because they are suffering from the boils."

"We've already been to several homes to relieve them in our patients," Puah reported.

Moses took a few shaky breaths and stared into the full vessel in his hand. "I fear what's coming," he agonized.

"What?"

"Tomorrow there will be a very grievous hail, the likes of which have not been seen in Egypt since it's foundations."

"Hail?" Eliora chocked on her bite of food.

"Is there any way to stop it?"

Moses slowly shook his head.

"Then we have much to prepare." Puah stood and handed Miriam her bowl. "Thank you for the meal, but we must leave."

"Of course. Anytime."

"But I'm not done," Eliora protested as her mentor pulled the bowl out of her hands and gave it also to their friend.

"Yes, you are. We have work to do." She gave a quick nod to Moses and hurried out of the gate.

"Thanks again." The young midwife bowed to them and rushed after her mentor. "Slow down!" she called. "Why are you in such a hurry?"

"If tomorrow is going to be as bad as Moses reports, we must make plans."

"Plans for what?" Eliora tripped trying to keep up.

"For the pregnant women in Egypt."

"I don't understand." Her breathing quickened. "Tell me what's going on and where are we heading."

It wasn't long before they turned down a street leading to the palace complex.

"Pharaoh's house?" Eliora asked.

Puah sped up as the building came into view.

"You're not going to try to speak to Pharaoh yourself, are you?"

"No."

The younger woman took in a deep breath and let it out.

"I'm going to see Queen Satiah."

"Why her?"

"I believe she can help."

Gaining entrance past the guards was not a problem this time for Puah. Though they did follow the women until reaching the queen.

"It is well," she reassured her royal protection. "They are welcome here."

The men bowed and returned to their post.

"Now, tell me what you have come for today?" She stepped lightly on the painted tile. "You look very much rattled."

"I'm afraid I am, my Queen." Breaths burned in her lungs as she spoke each word carefully. "I have a great favor to ask of you."

"Speak it."

"I request refuge for the pregnant women of Egypt."

The queen paused. "For what purpose?"

"To save them from certain destruction."

"Has there been a threat to their lives?"

"In a manner of speaking."

"I suggest you speak more specifically as you are treading on dangerous ground." She folded her hands across her body.

Puah straightened. "Forgive the cover of speech, but you know that Moses has been before your husband?"

"On numerous occasions now." She started walking again.

"The message he brought today was of a powerful plague heading toward Egypt on the morrow."

"We have had flies, frogs, boils, diseased cattle…what else could happen?"

"Hail."

"Hail?" She paused. "You are not serious."

"I am. A hailstorm is coming unlike any Egypt has ever seen."

"And your solution?"

"Bring as many women who are willing into the palace."

"Here?"

"Yes, my Queen," she offered. "The hail will only fall in the cities outside of Goshen. Unfortunately, we don't have the room or time to move them all that far north. We might just have enough time to bring them here. This is the most fortified building in all of Egypt."

The royal woman was quiet for some time before she gave her answer, "You say this will happen on the morrow?"

Puah nodded.

"Then I'll leave my guards at your disposal. My servants will prepare rooms here while you gather the women."

"Thank you." She bowed. "If you'll excuse us, we must move quickly. There isn't much time."

"Of course." She waved them off. "Hurry."

The two midwives rushed out of the palace and into the streets toward the south.

"Where to first?"

Puah huffed as she pushed her old body. "We need to find Layla. She can help us."

"Do you think she will?" Eliora lamented.

"All we can do is ask."

With only a few inquiries, they were able to locate Puah's Egyptian apprentice staying with another midwife.

"You got permission?" Layla questioned with her hands on her narrow hips.

"From the queen herself," Puah explained.

"Do you really think it's going to be so bad that this is necessary?"

"I do."

"What about the Hebrew women living in the south?" Eliora asked.

"I'm sure they will be welcomed in the palace as well."

"You want us to send a bunch of helpless women into the lion's den?" the young woman objected.

"We don't have time to argue over this."

"The royal family would not harm them," Layla protested.

"No. They would just have them sent to work."

"Peace, ladies." The older midwife raised her

arms. "We are wasting time with this bickering. I've gotten permission from the queen to move women tonight."

"How are we going to move them all?"

"That's why we're here. We need all the midwives we can. Hebrew and Egyptian alike to help us move the women. We'll send the Hebrew women into Goshen and bring the Egyptian women into the palace. If we have to, we'll work all night."

"I think the real question is, how do we convince them to go?"

She opened her mouth and then shut it again. "We can't. We can only offer."

Chapter 16

"So there was hail, and fire mingled with the hail, very grievous, such as there was none like it in all the land of Egypt since it became a nation."
-EXODUS 9:24

It had taken all night, but every willing woman had been moved. Hebrews to open homes in Goshen. Egyptians into the palace. The midwife guild had once again come to the rescue. Each woman used every ounce of strength to assure the safety of their patients and families.

Puah collapsed on a soft couch just as the rays of morning light bathed the only empty room in the palace with brightness and warmth.

"We did it." Eliora melted down at her feet. She raised an arm to the couch and laid her head on her elbow.

"Yes." She closed her eyes. "We did."

It was only moments before Puah heard easy breathing coming from her apprentice. She opened her eyes just enough to watch the rhythmic movements of the younger girl's body. She smiled, closed her eyes again, and settled deeper into the welcoming fabric to join her in slumber.

Before she could fall into a deep sleep, the palace walls shook around them.

Puah sat straight up.

"What was that?" Eliora roused, obviously still half asleep.

"I don't know."

Another violent shake of the walls around her forced the mentor to her feet. "We need to check on the others."

The student wobbled to her unsteady legs. "Of course." She rubbed her eyes with her fists and followed.

They rushed up and down the halls poking their heads into each room of the many apartments. At some moments, they had to clutch a wall or doorway with the shaking.

Eliora dared a peek out a large window.

"Get away from there," Puah ordered.

"It's true." She pointed.

The mentor eased toward the opening and looked out.

Fire rained down from the sky in giant balls. Lightning crackled and thunder boomed from the ominous clouds covering the normally clear sky.

Puah grabbed Eliora's shoulders and moved her away. "Have everyone stay clear of the windows."

They searched the hallways again.

When another ferocious shake forced them to brace themselves against a nearby wall, Eliora screamed, "Do you think the palace walls will hold?"

"If any place in Egypt will, this will be it," she yelled back.

"Goddess Nut, please help us!" Neith cried as she ran by them.

"Maybe she's too far away to hear you." Eliora covered her ears and turned her back to the hallway. She put her head against the wall and waited for the shaking to subside.

Crashing sounds and screams mixed with cracking thunder outside the complex carried through the high windows in the next room.

"Come on." Puah grabbed her student's arm and moved her to a room.

"Shu hear our pleas!" Neith cried from a corner. She was huddled together with her legs drawn up to her body.

"Isn't he your calming god? This doesn't seem very calm to me."

"Eliora you are not helping the situation," Puah corrected. She pushed her into the hallway again to find a different room.

"They cry to gods with deaf ears instead of submitting to the One who would hear if they cried to Him." The younger woman spun away and threw her hands up. "What am I supposed to do?"

"Make yourself useful and check the women. All this stress could cause some to go into labor."

Eliora cut her eyes into the room where Neith was still crying out to any god she could think to name before she left to make a round.

Puah sighed and went to kneel beside her friend. "She doesn't mean any harm." She brushed the woman's long hair with her fingers. "She is simply young and outspoken."

"I'm going to go pray some more." Neith got up and walked toward the altar in the room. She lit some more incense and chanted.

"Good idea," Puah said to herself. She bent low to the tile floor and whispered prayers to the God raining fire down on her head.

"Puah!" Eliora rushed into the room.

The old woman lifted her gaze.

"Come quick."

She raised her stiff body and rushed after her student.

In another apartment, an Egyptian woman was in the late stages of labor.

"I knew this was going to happen." She bent under the woman. "Let's see how things are going."

The woman let out a wail.

"She's progressing quickly," the midwife reported. "Get me some clean linen and water mixed with wine. This one will be here soon."

In less than an hour, Puah held up the freshly wrapped bundle of a small Egyptian boy. "He is well."

"Thank you," the new mother breathed with relief.

"Rest. I'll be back to check in on you later."

"We've got another one across the hall," Layla called.

"Maybe if this keeps up all the women will deliver tonight," Eliora teased. "Then perhaps you and I can take a break for a few months."

A violent rattle that felt as if the entire palace was being moved caused them to stop in the hallway for a moment.

"A midwife's work is never done, my young apprentice."

When the shaking settled, the two went into the next room to help welcome another life into the world.

Late into the night, a total of five new sets of lungs breathed their first breaths of air.

Puah laid down somewhere in the dark. Exhaustion had caught up with her until she couldn't hold her eyes open any longer. The sounds of destruction still rained outside, but sleep clawed at her. She found an empty corner where she curled herself into a ball on the cool tile and closed her eyes.

Sometime later, she was roused with a shake.

The sounds of the hail storm still raged outside the protective walls of the palace.

When her eyes adjusted to the flickers of lamplight, she looked into a familiar face. "My Queen." She stirred. "What's wrong?"

"Pharaoh Thutmose III has called for Moses and Aaron," Queen Satiah whispered.

"Why?"

"I don't know."

"They wouldn't come through all this," Eliora insisted from somewhere in the darkness.

"He sent guards to fetch them. They will come."

"Can we stand witness?" Puah rubbed her eyes and yawned.

She nodded. "That's why I came to find you. They should be back soon."

Moses and Aaron walked into the throne room within the hour.

"I have sinned this time. Your God is righteous and I and my people are wicked. Plead to the Lord for this is enough." Pharaoh rubbed his temples. "Ask him to stop the hail and I will let you go."

"As soon as I reach the edge of the city," Moses said. "I will spread my hands out toward the Lord and the hail will cease. I will do this so you will know that the earth is the Lord's."

Pharaoh's mouth twisted into a short grin.

"But as for you and your people, I know that you will not yet fear the Lord."

His lips fell into a straight line.

The brothers turned their backs and marched out of the room.

"Do you think he can do it?" Eliora asked Puah as they made their way into the hallway.

"God has listened to him so far. I'm more concerned about what waits for us outside."

The apprentice scrunched her forehead.

"Not everyone will escape God's wrath."

Eliora's eyes widened with realization. "Oh no."

"You thought a full night of delivering babies was tough."

"I'll gather some supplies."

When silence finally fell in the palace, Eliora and Puah exchanged a grim glance.

"Waiting is not going to make it any easier."

The student threw another bag over her already loaded body. "I'm as ready as I'll ever be."

Reaching the front gate, Puah pushed it open and stepped onto the sandy street. Her eyes searched through stirred up dust clouds.

Fire blazed in every direction. Blood stained the sand. Bodies lay everywhere. Smoke rose from piles of rubble where proud buildings once stood. Homes stood half upright but mostly destroyed. Trees were left broken in pieces.

"Where do we start?" Eliora stood frozen at the gateway.

"Put out those flames," Pharaoh ordered from

behind them.

Several units of guards rushed past the women and started fighting the fires.

Eliora tightened her grip on the strap of one of her bags. She rushed toward the nearest body. Pulling out a bandage from the satchel, she applied pressure to one of his lacerations. "Hold still," she spoke softly to the man who stirred under her touch.

Puah hurried to aid someone else. She quickly pressed a clean linen to the gushing wound on his head. "We need to send word into Goshen," she called to her apprentice. "Our midwives can offer aid."

"How do we do that?" Eliora yelled back as she moved to another body to check for life and then injuries.

"Your people are the cause of all this." Pharaoh stood over Puah and narrowed his gaze. "I should send each and every one of you to labor in my quarries until you fall where you stand."

She stood up to face him. "Would you rather your people continue to lie bleeding in your streets?"

He huffed.

"My people can help. My guild is trained in medical aid. If I call, they will come and help."

He ground his teeth and turned away.

"You need us."

He stopped. "Fine." He picked up his pace

again. "Guard!"

A royal patrol officer hurried to him. "Yes, Mighty Pharaoh?"

"Send word to Goshen. Call the midwives."

"Sir?"

"You heard me." He pushed the man's bare chest away. "I said go. Now!"

The guard ran as fast as he could toward the north.

Puah bent down to check the pressure on the bandage she had just tied. "We are going to need a place to organize help."

"Bring them into the palace." Queen Satiah offered, appearing beside her.

Pharaoh's shape vanished in the dense smoke.

"It's the least we can do for our people." She shook her head looking down at the man, Puah was working on. "More of them should have listened to you."

"At least many are safe inside already."

"But many more are out here. Who knows how many will need aid. Or have lost everything."

"We'll know by the end of the day."

"I'll get my cooks preparing more food and pallets for those without homes."

"We'll need some of your strongest guards to carry these bigger men inside too."

"I shall send as many as you need." The queen disappeared into the gates of the palace.

"Puah," Eliora's voice beckoned from down

the street.

Running in her direction, she came to a halt when she noticed Eliora bent over a body. "We've got more supplies coming."

"They're not going to help her."

She came around to look into the face of the person her student was hunched over.

Dark, lifeless, yet familiar eyes stared back at her.

"Ouei." She collapsed beside the body. "I tried to talk her into coming inside."

"We all did," Eliora comforted.

She reached over and forced the woman's eyes closed. "Rest." As she moved her hand away from the woman's face, her palm came to rest on the woman's rounded stomach. "I'm sorry we didn't get to meet, little one."

Eliora's eyes watered. "Look." She pointed to another unresponsive body lying nearby. "One of her cows. She was so worried about bringing them inside when her husband refused to obey the word of God. She must have gotten caught out here when the hail started trying to bring them back."

"Come on," Puah ordered. "Let's help the ones we can."

Moments before sunset, the palace was filled to capacity with injured or displaced bodies.

"There are so many of them," Eliora commented as her eyes searched the huddled groups of people.

"I'm glad we got the majority of our people into Goshen yesterday. This place couldn't hold anymore."

"Where do we start?"

"We just start."

Chapter 17

"And the LORD said unto Moses, 'Stretch out thine hand over the land of Egypt for the locusts, that they may come up upon the land of Egypt, and eat every herb of the land, even all that the hail hath left.' "
-EXODUS 10:12

As the month of Edar drew to a close, Puah and Eliora made their way toward the home of Sofh. They had helped the Egyptian women return to their homes after the hail storm. Many Hebrews chose to stay in Goshen with family or friends. Everyone's guard remained up not knowing when or what the next plague would be.

Layla had decided to split her time between Goshen and the home of another midwife in the south. She rotated between the two every few weeks.

Sofh's buildings suffered extensive damage in the hail storm, but she had enlisted her many servants to work repairing the damage. Reconstruction was nearly complete.

"We brought you grain from Goshen." Puah handed Sofh a bag of barley.

She wrinkled her nose. "I'm sure we'll be fine. The wheat and spelt are beginning to ripen. Their sprouts were not ruined by the storm."

The midwife pulled the offer back into herself. "If you insist."

"Can we get this check over quickly? I have much work to tend to."

"I hope you're not doing too much work. Your body needs rest as well to prepare for delivery."

The women worked quickly to examine their patient and then left her to her duties.

"Puah," Layla bowed as she approached them on the way. "I've been searching for you."

"Another patient?"

"No, it's Miriam. She came to call on you while you were away."

"Is she ill?"

"No. She said Moses had been before Pharaoh this morning."

"That doesn't sound good," Eliora urged.

"Let us make haste then."

"Not me. I'm staying as far away from the palace as possible." Layla turned around and walked away.

The other two midwives ran towards the home of Aaron.

They were greeted by the warm smile of Miriam. "So good of you to come."

"Tell me what help we can be?" Puah offered.

"It's Moses."

"An audience with Pharaoh?"

She nodded. "This one has gotten him very upset." She pointed. "He's up there."

"I'll see to him." The older midwife climbed the ladder to the upper room. "Moses?" she called into the chamber.

"Here I am," he answered.

"Your sister sent me to check on you." She stepped into the room but stayed in the doorway. "Are you ill?"

"If only that were the case. It would be easy to remedy with a bit of medicine." He crossed the room to step into the sunlight. "Though I'm afraid this illness can't be cured so readily."

"I'm told you've been to see Pharaoh again."

"The reason for my distress."

She waited for him to continue.

"You think he would have listened after the hail storm knocked out most of his beloved cities and a few Egyptians as well."

"Another plague is coming?" she guessed.

He nodded somberly. "I told him that if he continued to refuse to humble himself before God, then tomorrow there will be a swarm of locusts unlike any of their generations had seen."

"What did he say?"

"We left him to think it over."

"An army that large can eat more than a few

thousand of us can eat in a day. They'll ruin the remaining crops for sure."

"I know. Their people will starve."

Puah thought. "I can use my guild to spread more food. I'm just not sure how far our resources can stretch."

"Moses?" Miriam called from the bottom of the ladder. "A royal guard is here for you."

Moses and Puah crawled down the ladder to meet Aaron and Eliora at the bottom.

"Guess the verdict is in," Aaron said, grabbing his staff.

Puah and her apprentice followed the two men to the palace.

"You may go into the wilderness to serve your God," Pharaoh Thutmose III spoke clear and with no emotion.

Moses breathed a sigh of relief.

"But who do you expect to take with you?"

"Our young and old. Our sons and daughters. All our herds and flocks, for we must hold a feast unto the Lord."

Pharaoh smoothed down his dark beard. "Your men can go, but let your children stay. The wilderness is no place for young ones. If you have a need to go serve your Lord, then go out and serve Him. Just leave your children here to protect them from harm." He waved them off.

Moses and Aaron were shoved out of the palace once again.

"I grow weary of being removed from somewhere I don't wish to be in the first place." Aaron dusted off his robe and straightened it.

Moses marched down the street and into an open field.

"What are you going to do?" Puah asked following him.

"The Lord says it's time." He stopped and stretched his rod over the land.

In the same moment, a mighty wind kicked up from the east.

She shielded her face with her arms. "Is this the next plague?" she shouted over the rushing squall.

"No," he bellowed. "But it will carry it."

Later that night, Puah lay on her straw mat in the middle of her home. The wind hadn't ceased howling since it began. She twisted to her side and listened to a loose flap bang somewhere in the dark.

God of the universe. I don't know what's coming, but help me sleep tonight so I can be prepared for it in the morning. You've given me charge over pregnant women and their children. Allow me rest so that I may serve You by serving them. Expand our resources like you did for Joseph when he helped saved Egypt from the coming famine.

As the sunlight warmed her face and caused her to wake the following morning, Puah opened her eyes to the stillness.

She found Eliora in the kitchen fixing a plate of dried fruit. "How did you sleep?"

"Not as well as I would have liked."

"That wind was awful." She handed a plate to her. "Why would Moses choose wind? It doesn't seem very powerful and has since stopped."

Puah popped a shriveled fig in her mouth. "God brought it, but I see your point."

"I don't think that was a very effective plague."

She tossed another piece over her lips. "The wind wasn't the plague. He said it was going to carry it."

"Who knows what awaits us out there today?" Eliora picked off her own plate.

Only You, Lord. Puah thought to herself.

When they finished their breakfast, the two women gathered supplies and headed to their first stop.

As the gate swung open in front of them, a mound of locusts poured forth.

Eliora picked up her feet and shook one from her sandal. "I think we just discovered the next plague."

"They're eating everything we have left," the servant said, climbing over the stack of pests. "You can't take a step without treading on one of these creatures." She pulled two from her hair.

They made their way through the city checking on as many women as they could. Some could not open their doors because of the load of locusts that filled their homes.

"After we check in on this patient," Eliora said in the middle of a pile of insects. "I think we need to go find Moses."

"Agreed."

Aaron's wife, Elisheba, had pointed them in the direction of the palace where Puah and Eliora found themselves listening in on another interaction between the brothers.

"I have sinned against the Lord your God and against you. Forgive me," Pharaoh pleaded. "Intreat the Lord this last time that He will take away this certain death from my people."

Moses didn't even bother to respond. He simply turned away and walked out of the room.

The two midwives followed him for a long time until he stopped near the Red Sea.

Stretching his hands out, he prayed. As he did, a mighty wind kicked up from the west.

"Look." Eliora pointed. "They are being driven into the sea."

Mounds and mounds of locust were pushed from the land into the waters.

Moses stood there with his arms outstretched until every one of them was tossed into the sea by the wind.

When the last one hit the water, he dropped his arms and marched toward his home.

"Why don't you join us for the evening meal?"

Miriam offered. "It's been a long day for all of us."

The women filled the home with savory aromas while Moses and Aaron spoke in hushed tones in the courtyard.

"My husband is growing quite irate from all this," Elisheba noted. "I'm afraid his long run of patience is quickly growing dim."

"I wonder how much longer Pharaoh's tolerance will be for our people," Eliora said, stirring the stew.

A knock at the gate made all of them hold their breaths.

Moses rose to answer the door. He held the gate open only briefly before closing it. Then he spoke to Aaron before heading for the ladder.

"Again?" Aaron complained and chased after him.

Moses stopped on the second rung. "Yes. He has recanted his offer."

"This is getting to be too much. How much longer are we to endure this Pharaoh?" His voice trailed off as they climbed into the upper room.

Elisheba looked toward the ceiling. "God grant me more endurance."

Zipporah filled a bowl and handed it to Puah before doing the same for each of the young ones.

"May He grant it to all of us," the old woman added.

"From your lips to God's ears," Zipporah clasped her hands together. "I don't know how much more I can take."

Chapter 18

"And the LORD said unto Moses, 'Stretch out thine hand toward heaven, that there may be darkness over the land of Egypt, even darkness which may be felt.' "
-EXODUS 10:21

The beginning of Nisan had always been Puah's favorite time of year. She remembered as a child watching the new flowers bloom and enjoying the sweet scents they brought with them.

These days she hardly had a moment to stop and appreciate life. The recent years had flown by and she didn't have many left ahead. The current months had heightened everyone's emotions. People she counted as friends or at least friendly, stared at her out of the corners of their eyes. It was as if every Hebrew carried the fault of the plagues on their shoulders. Egyptians were being singled out for Pharaoh's pride and they hated the Hebrews for it.

Lying on her straw mat, she inhaled deeply hoping to catch a sweet and soothing scent, but none was to be found. The locusts had devoured every green thing in their path. She whispered a prayer of thanks that Eliora had woven a new sleeping mat for her just before the hail storm.

It would be months before the new seeds would take root and bloom. If there were any left to have a fighting chance.

She shook her thoughts away. There was too much to do to focus on results she couldn't control. She rose, washed, and spread out the materials of her craft to prepare for the day.

The creaking of the gate opening interrupted her packing. She made her way into the courtyard to see who was calling at such an early hour before she had time to finish packing her bag. Upon seeing Eliora's young face, her frustration was washed away.

"Where have you been?" Puah waved her young apprentice inside.

"I headed out early to get some fresh food, but it's getting scarce in Egypt," Eliora answered as she closed the door behind herself and moved to place her satchel on the table in the kitchen. "We might have to plan a trip into Goshen soon to stock up." She eyed the supplies on the table. "Did someone come calling already?"

"No. I couldn't sleep, so I was just trying to get an early start for the day." She double checked the items already in the bag and went to work packing the others.

"Are you uneasy?"

"Is it that obvious?"

"I know you better than you think."

"You weren't going to leave without me, were you?" she asked, trying unsuccessfully to hide her hurt.

Puah paused and looked into the dark eyes of the younger woman. "I was going to search for you as soon as I finished packing."

The apprentice's face eased slightly.

"Help me make sure I have everything," she said, returning to her work. "We need to visit Sofh again. She is due any day now."

"Oh." Eliora rolled her eyes. "Is the baby positioned right?"

"Not the last time I checked and with this being her first delivery, it is not going to be easy." Puah shook her head.

The young girl stretched out her hand and placed it on the older woman's arm. "What is really making you so nervous? You have delivered hundreds of babies and I've never seen you so shaken."

She searched the face of her young counterpart before saying, "I fear more plagues and if the pattern continues..."

"I can't imagine anything worse than what we've already witnessed."

Her face hardened. "That is what I am afraid of. I don't believe we have seen the worst."

There was a long, worried pause.

"Let's make some rounds in Goshen and fill our supplies. Most of the women are still there from the hail storm. On our way back home, we'll stop to check on Sofh. Maybe visiting a few Hebrew's will encourage your heart enough to have patience with her." She placed two packed bags on each of her shoulders.

"Can I help you carry anything?" the girl asked, trying to take some burden off her mentor.

"Sure." Puah handed her a bag.

The two women took their time with each of their patients checking not only the health of the pregnancies but the well-being of the mothers. As they made their way south out of Goshen, they stopped to check on their last remaining Egyptian patients.

Against her better judgment, Puah had agreed to let Layla oversee the Egyptian midwives in the major cities of the south while she and Eliora trained the Hebrew midwives of the north. After the last few plagues, many of the Hebrew women had left the major cities to find refuge in the land of Goshen. Witnessing the abundant provision of the fertile land and lack of plagues caused many of them to stay.

She was glad her people were well taken care of and it made her rounds easier to perform with many of them close together. Though her heart mourned the breaking of the system her mentor had set up. The teams of midwives she knew and loved included one well-trained mentor who had two apprentices. One Hebrew and one Egyptian, working side by side to help women throughout the entire country. The division felt wrong and unnatural to her. She longed to see alliance in her guild once again.

She left instructions with Layla that if any Egyptian woman was found lacking food, to send word to the midwives in Goshen to fill the need. She had hoped the gesture of sharing would bring them all back together again. To Puah's knowledge, no Egyptian had accepted the offer.

Her mind bustled with other ideas to bring them together again when they made it to the gate of Sofh's home.

Eliora knocked and waited.

The young servant girl they'd come to pity answered the door.

"Greetings, Aria," Puah smiled. "We're here to see Sofh."

"Come in. She has been expecting you. I believe the pains are growing closer together." She closed the door behind them. "She has been screaming orders all morning to the point she has driven away most of the others. They will be back later. I hope."

Aria moved a curtain back to reveal her sleeping mistress. "I believe she passed out from the pain."

"It happens," Puah said, trying to lighten the servant's tension. "I need to check her. Aria, will you start preparing us some room and get me a few clean linens."

"Right away." The servant bowed and then left to accomplish her tasks.

The midwife made her way over to the sleeping woman.

"Are you just going to check her while she still sleeps?" Eliora asked.

"She does need to rest, but I need to see how close this baby is to coming."

As Puah stretched out her hand to rouse the sleeping woman, everything went dark.

Aria screamed from somewhere in the house.

The loud noise startled Sofh who lurched up and into Puah.

"Easy, Sofh," the midwife whispered as she held the frightened and struggling woman in her arms.

"Puah?" Eliora called from close by.

"I am here," she said as she laid the sobbing woman back down on her bed.

"What has happened?" Sofh wept.

"I'm not sure. Just lay still." She patted the woman's arm. "Eliora, can you make it to the door and try to get some light in here?"

The girl slowly made her way toward the direction she thought she remembered they came in.

"Aria?" she called.

"I am here, but I am not sure where here is exactly," the servant girl confessed.

"Take it slow and follow the sound of my voice," Puah instructed.

A loud thud told her that Aria had knocked something over on her way toward them.

"Don't worry about cleaning that up. I need you. Get down on your hands and knees and feel your way over here." She guided her. "That's right. Nice and easy."

Just as Aria made her way to Puah's leg, Eliora yelled, "I think I found the door."

"Good. Open it and get us some light. Any light." She reached down to help the girl stand.

"Puah, the door is open and it's even darker out in the streets than in here. I can't see anything."

"Something's not right," the mentor said more to herself. "Aria, do you know where there are any oil lamps close by."

"I think I can find some."

"Careful, take it slow," she warned the younger woman as she turned her attention back to the weeping lady beside her. "Sofh, I know you're frightened right now, but I need to check on your baby. I'm going to adjust you into position. Try to stay calm for me."

She slowly moved the pregnant body from her side to her back. She felt around her midsection to feel the position of the baby inside. At that moment, she whispered a prayer of thanks that this particular part of her job did not require sight as much as it did her knowledgeable fingers.

"Good. Now I'm going to see how far along you are. Just take a few deep breaths and stay calm."

The older woman slightly raised Sofh's legs and measured the path the baby would take.

"All done for now." She wiped her fingers on her dress." Try to relax and sleep some more."

"Puah," Eliora whispered as she found her mentor in the dark.

"Yes, it is me. Take my hand and step slowly with me for a moment."

The two women took a few cautious steps away from the bed.

"How is she?" Eliora whispered in Puah's ear.

"The baby has moved slightly since the last time I came to check, but not in the exact position as of yet.," she whispered back. "The problem is she is progressing rapidly, which means this baby is going to come soon."

"How long do you think this darkness will last?"

She shook her head. "I have no idea, but we need to prepare for this baby with or without light."

"What's the plan?"

"I'll find my bag. You find Aria. See if she has

discovered any lamps yet and help her find the linens too."

Eliora squeezed Puah's hand. "I think you were right."

"About what?"

"This is much worse."

She nodded. "Go now and meet me back at the bed as soon as you can."

Both women bent their knees and moved their hands in front of themselves to keep from stumbling in the darkness.

Eliora half walked half crawled until her feet bumped into something. The pile was whimpering. "Aria, is that you?"

Her small form was heaving on the floor.

"Aria?"

"It is I," she said through sobs. "I am sorry I cannot help. I can't do it."

"What are you talking about?"

"The lamps…the lamps…"

Puah heard something scrape on the tile floor.

"They won't light. I've tried every way I know how," the servant whined.

"Are they out of oil?" Eliora asked as she searched for the object in the dark.

"No, they're full." She shook the container.

Eliora could hear the oil sloshing inside. Her fingers brushed the cool clay as she grabbed the lamp. She shook it to confirm that it was indeed full of oil. "Give me the fire starters."

Aria held out the two rocks.

She hit them together as fast as she could, but there was not even a hint of a spark.

"I've tried, I've tried. It should be working, but I couldn't get anything." The girl began to weep again.

She rubbed and rubbed with no success. "I don't understand any of this. We should be able to see something by now, but I still can't even see my hand in front of my face." She let out a frustrating grunt. "Well, Puah needs us. We need to bring her supplies. Get up." She nudged Aria. "Show me where there are some clean linens."

Aria took a moment to wipe her face and then she rolled from her side onto her hands and knees as she crawled away.

A few moments later, Eliora and Aria found their way to the bed where Puah was waiting for them.

"Here's what we could find." The servant placed the linens next to Puah's leg.

"Thank you. How is the search for light going?"

"That is the bad news," Eliora answered. "We found lamps, but we cannot get anything lit. It's the strangest thing."

"Is the door still opened?"

"Yes, I left it open."

"I guess no one else can get anything lit then either because there is still no outside light."

"A plague?" Aria gasped.

"Yes, the ninth," the mentor agreed. "A plague of darkness. God is in this. He has kept the light away. For how long, I do not know."

At that moment, Sofh's scream of pain brought them back to the task at hand.

Puah rubbed the young woman's arm as she grasped her midsection.

"Well, ladies, we have a baby coming. Let's get to it," the older midwife reminded them. "Aria, unfold those linens and place them in a pile near me on the bed. Eliora, help me get Sofh into position. I need to try something."

The women all moved as cautiously, but swiftly as they could in the heavy darkness.

"Good. Ladies, each of you get under Sofh's arms and hold her steady. Sofh, I know you want to push, but I need you not to right now. I don't think your baby is in the right position yet. I need to twist the baby around. It's going to hurt, but I have to in order to help you deliver properly. Do you understand me? Do NOT push until I say."

Sofh screamed again in pain and began to sob.

"I'll take that as a yes."

Puah placed both of her slim hands on top of the woman's round belly and began to push the baby inside. In response, the baby kicked and adjusted. Again, she pressed Sofh's stomach trying to coax the baby inside to move into the correct position.

"Almost there," she said as she fingered the flesh to measure where the young one was located. "Sofh, I need you to take a deep breath because I need to press harder."

Sofh inhaled as Puah pressed hard on one side of the mother's stomach. A large exhale was choked with a scream of pain.

"There," the skilled midwife said as she felt the baby move just where she planned. "Now, on the next pain I need you to go ahead and push so we can get this baby out."

Sofh took a few deep breaths.

"That's right, take your time and focus on your breathing," Puah calmed her patient. "Eliora, Aria, hold tight to her arms. It is almost time to push."

The two women on either side tensed their grip.

"Push, Sofh."

The woman screamed through the pain as she bore down.

"Good girl. Now, take another few deep breaths and then we are going to push again," she said as she reached over to the pile of linens beside her foot and wrapped a few around her hands in preparation for the slippery newborn.

Sofh began to whine.

"Okay, time to push again. Oh, I can feel the head. Your baby is almost here. Keep pushing."

Another large exhale as Sofh stopped. "I'm

tired. I don't want to push anymore. Just pull it out."

"You know I can't do that. Come now, just another push or two and your baby will be in your arms." Puah slid her slim fingers around the baby's head to help ease its way out of its mother's body. "Push!"

The woman bore down hard while Puah gently guided the newborn into the world.

Sofh exhaled a long breath as she collapsed back into the two women who were supporting her.

The midwife wiped the wiggly baby in the pure darkness with clean linens and then felt the tiny body to check as best she could to make sure the baby was healthy.

"Everything feels fine. Of course, I cannot see anything," she said as her fingers made their way over the small baby one more time. A broad smile crossed her face. "Congratulations, it's a boy."

"A boy," the mother panted.

"Yes, a healthy boy."

"Well done," Eliora said as she and Aria helped Sofh slowly make her way back to the bed and eased her down.

"Eliora, come close to me."

The woman obeyed as quickly as she could in the pressing darkness.

"Take him to his mother, she needs to nurse as soon as possible," Puah said as she slowly transferred the baby into Eliora's arms. "Easy now, he is a wiggler."

"Of course," the student said as she accepted the baby and then went back to Sofh's side.

Puah went to work cleaning Sofh. She reached into her nearby bag and began to pull out her bottles of herbs. Having to rely on her sense of smell, she opened each one until she found the herbs she needed.

"Whenever we get some light, I'll be able to make a better mix, but for now this will have to do," she whispered to herself as she worked.

"There now, just like that," Eliora instructed the new mother as she used her hands to guide the baby to his mother's waiting breast.

The sound of happy suckling gave all the women in the room a wash of peace and contentment.

"Have you decided on a name?" Puah asked after a few moments of enjoying the sweet sounds of new life.

The mother thought for a time. "Mesu," she said simply. "My son."

"Good choice," Eliora said with a smile and a single tear in her eye.

Chapter 19

"But the LORD hardened Pharaoh's heart, and he would not let them go."
-EXODUS 10:27

After three days of caring for a newborn baby boy and his mother without the help of eyesight, Puah and Eliora were worn out. It had taken most of their time and energy to learn to navigate the large house in the dark and find their way around mostly by crawling on the cold tile floors.

Aria had been a great help to the two midwives since none of Sofh's other servants were able to find their way back to the house due to the darkness.

The streets remained eerily quiet the entire three days because anyone who left the safety of the building they were in risked losing all direction.

Puah kept everyone calm and spent much of the time next to Sofh teaching her about motherhood, taking care of a newborn, as well as taking care of herself.

The mother spent much of the three days nuzzling her newborn and repeating how much she wished she could see his face.

The odd discovery that during the whole time no one could see even their own hand pressed against their nose took the first two days to get over. By the third day, they were beginning to wonder if this was going to be their new way of life.

"It has to end sometime," Puah reassured them. "All the other plagues ended at some point. This too will pass when God decides to let it."

The Egyptian women were not as sure as Puah seemed to be about the God of the Hebrews, but He had certainly put doubts in their minds about the gods they worshipped.

"Tell us another story," Aria asked in her childish voice.

"Oh yes, please," Eliora pleaded. "Tell us another story."

"Well, there is not much else to do is there?" She resigned to entertain the bored women. "Let me see, which one have I not told yet?" The older woman rubbed her chin. "Ah, I will tell you the one about the great flood."

She heard a slight rustling sound as the three women made themselves comfortable around her to hear the story.

"Once there was a man named Noah who had

three sons. One day, God called Noah to build a very large enclosed boat because He was going to make it rain and rain a lot."

"At least we have not had a plague of rain," Sofh said harshly.

"Not yet," Aria said.

"Quiet you two, I want to hear the story," Eliora corrected.

"Well, you see," the mentor continued. "It had never rained before, so the people did not know what rain was. But by faith, Noah followed all God's instructions even while other people made fun of him. God gave Noah the exact plans to build this large boat and He called it an ark. It took Noah 120 years to build this massive project."

"Do you think this darkness will last 120 years?" the servant asked.

"I do not know," she said slowly. "Only God knows."

"I hope not," the apprentice added.

Puah picked up her story, "When Noah was finished building, God told him to collect two of every animal and place them inside the boat. God put it in the hearts of all the animals to go to Noah and gather inside the boat. He also put peace in their hearts so they would not eat each other while they rode together. After the animals were on the boat, Noah gathered his family. His wife, their three sons, and their sons' wives. When they were all safe and sound on the boat, God shut the door of the ark."

"And then it rained?" the servant girl asked.

"Well, not at first. God waited a few days before He made it rain. But when the rains came, it flooded the entire world so much so that every person who was not in the ark drowned."

"I don't know if I would trust this God of wrath," Sofh said, adjusting her son from one arm to the other. "He seems to be more of a punisher than Meretseger."

She continued as she ignored the comment, "It rained all day and night for forty days and then it finally stopped. Noah waited in the ark until the dry land appeared again and God made the ark land on top of a mountain. When everyone got out of the boat, Noah made an altar and worshipped God for protecting his family and saving the lives of the animals. God put colors in the sky in the shape of a bow and then promised Noah that He would never flood the world like that again."

"I like that story," Aria said happily.

"I do not," Sofh said with a huff.

"What do you think, Eliora?" the servant asked, trying to be respectful of her master, yet ignore her at the same time.

"I've never really understood the story. What does it mean, Puah?"

"God does punish those who do wrong like when He flooded the world to cause their deaths, but He also gave them a way out of the punishment. For 120 years, as Noah built the ark, he talked about God with all who would listen. They were given a long time to follow God and do what He asked them to do, but no one outside of Noah's family got on the boat.

"So, the story teaches me that the God of the Hebrews is very longsuffering and wants people to obey Him, but that He is not going to wait around forever for us to make up our minds. God protected all those animals and Noah's family in the ark and they got to live and go on with their lives after the flood. I think when God tells us to do something, then we better obey so we don't get caught up in the punishment."

"I wish Pharaoh would have listened to the God of the Hebrews," the servant commented. "This darkness is beginning to really make me sad."

In that same moment, all the women were blinded by a great light that filled the room.

Screams of fear and frustration escaped from their mouths at once as they all had to cover their eyes from the blinding light.

"Ra has been delivered," Sofh said with glee.

"Finally!" Eliora said as she jumped up with joy. She put her hands in front of her face. "I can see again!"

Puah rubbed her aching eyes and blinked several times.

The student made her way to the front door

and opened it wide. "The warmth feels so good," she said as she stood just outside the door and lifted her face toward the sun.

"I wish to feel it too," Aria said as she ran toward the open door.

Puah stretched out her legs from underneath herself when she peered over to Sofh and young Mesu. "Why are you crying, my dear?" she asked the woman.

Sniffling, the woman answered, "He is so beautiful!" The mother gazed at the face of the son she had borne three days before.

The midwife rose and walked to them. She leaned over to see the face of the little boy she had helped bring into the world a few days prior. "He is lovely. You should be proud." She smiled at the smooth face of the boy who reminded her of another baby boy she helped birth several decades before.

Sofh kissed Mesu's forehead over and over again. "Be blessed, my son, for you have brought your mother much joy."

Puah's mind wandered back to the night she helped Jochebed birth her third child. Moses had been the most beautiful baby she had ever seen and now he was a bold man who feared no one, not even Pharaoh. Right then, Puah decided she needed to find Moses as soon as she was done helping Sofh get settled. She had some questions for the man who she once held in her arms.

Mesu's cries brought her back to the present and she watched the new mother nurse her hungry baby.

"I've never been so happy to journey in the streets," Eliora said, practically dancing as they left Sofh's.

Puah smiled. "It does feel good to move without fear of falling in the darkness."

"I thought I had permanently lost my sight."

"You?" the mentor asked. "I'm the old woman here. When the light went out, I thought I had finally gone blind."

After a short visit with the women of Aaron's home, Puah found Moses on the roof.

"He said we could take our children, right?" she questioned him.

"That was his first offer, yes."

"Then why are you worried about the herds?" She threw her arms up in the air. "He said we can all go. The herds will be safe until we return."

"We need them to use as sacrifices," he explained. "It doesn't make any sense to go all the way out there with nothing to offer. I don't know exactly which ones God will require until we get there."

"I don't understand the issue," Puah said.

"We've done well serving God here in Egypt. Why do we need to go out into the wilderness to make sacrifices?"

"We are to leave Egypt completely. This is what God has commanded us to do."

"This is what God has commanded *you* to do." She pointed her finger at him as if she were correcting a small child.

"When will you try again?" Eliora interrupted as she stepped onto the rooftop.

"I'm not." Moses shrugged.

"You're done asking?" The young woman asked.

He shook his head. "Pharaoh has given orders that if I try to come before him again, he'll have me killed."

"So, we can put this behind us now and stop all these plagues?" Puah asked. "Innocent people are being harmed."

"None of us are innocent in God's eyes. He alone is holy and we are not."

"But this is the end of it?"

He shook his head gravely. "Pharaoh is right that I won't stand before him again, but not because of his order."

"Not another plague."

"Yes. Just one more."

"We've destroyed their river, their crops, and their deities," the student said. "What else is left for us to take from them?"

Moses sighed. "Their sons."

"What?" Puah took a step toward him. "What are you saying?"

"My heart is pained for the people of Egypt and all those who do not heed this final warning."

"Speak clearer."

"A plague of death to the first-born sons and their herds."

"How could you?" Puah turned away and rushed down the steps and out of the home.

Miriam found her later by the banks of a vein of the Nile. "May I join you?"

Puah nodded and wiped her wet face. "Did *he* send you?"

"No." She sat on the sandy shore. "I was worried about you. Eliora is too. She is searching all the homes of your patients."

Miriam allowed the silence to hang like a curtain between them.

Puah sniffled and wiped her face again. "Pharaoh Thutmose I ordered me to kill newborn Hebrew males. How can our God kill Egyptian firstborn males and their livestock? Isn't this the evil He is trying to stop? Not repeat?"

"I'm not going to sit here and pretend to have your answers."

"Then why did you come?"

The sister looked out over the calm waters. "I don't remember much, but I remember when Moses was born. I remember how scared Mother looked when Shiphrah told her she was going to take him away."

The older woman turned toward her.

"But she wasn't frightened at all the day she put him in the river. My mother had never been more determined in her whole life."

"She was a strong woman," Puah remarked.

"Do you know why?"

She shook her head.

"Because she trusted God with the results."

"Like when she put your brother in the river?" the midwife asked.

"Like that. She put in the hard work of preparing the basket. She hid him for three months before that. But her faith shone brightest when she placed that little ark in the reeds and let God handle the outcome."

"What are you trying to say?"

"I'm saying that we might not understand why God is choosing this plague. Maybe it's the only thing that will break Pharaoh. Only God knows his heart. Our job isn't to tell God His job. Our job is to trust Him with the outcome."

Puah was quiet for a long time contemplating Miriam's words. When she finally spoke, her voice was low and thoughtful, "I love the Egyptians almost as much as my own people. I've been trained to heal and bring life. How can I pitch my tent with a God who is destroying these people and bringing death?"

"No one can force you to do anything. In the end, it'll be your choice."

"I stood with Shiphrah in the path of a self-proclaimed god and we ended up saving hundreds of babies. For the past several months, I've been giving aid to the Egyptians through all these plagues. How can I sit by and let our God kill their children? And if I leave Egypt, I'll be leaving these people behind in their greatest hour of need. It goes against everything I've been called to do."

"Obedience isn't always easy."

"No, it's not." She dipped her chin to her chest.

"But it's always better to do things God's way." Miriam rose. "I think you should pray."

"I don't know if I could speak to God right now."

"That's exactly why you should." She faced north and left.

Puah looked to the clear blue sky. "God of the universe…" she faltered. "God, I'm pretty angry with You right now. I don't understand how You could kill when You've taught us it's wrong to murder." She sighed. "I love both these groups of people. I want to serve the way You've called me. I also know that I could never instruct You in Your ways. You don't need a mentor. So, if this is Your plan, then help me obey and trust You with the results."

A gentle breeze blew hair away from her face.

She rose and shook the sand from her dress. With confusion still churning inside her, she made her way back to Aaron's home.

"I'm ready to obey," she announced as she let herself into the open courtyard.

"Do you understand what this means?" Moses came to her.

"I don't believe I ever fully will, but I know our God is bigger than anything," Puah said with conviction. "And I'm ready to trust Him with the results."

Miriam grinned from the doorway of the kitchen.

Moses thought for a moment. "God has given each a choice. If you choose to obey, you will be welcomed to join us."

"Thank you." She bowed.

"Don't thank me yet. It will not be easy and there is still one more plague to survive."

"I don't understand this last one," she said with caution.

"What is man that he can understand the mind of God?"

She let the words sink into her soul. They weren't what she wanted to hear, but she knew they were what God wanted to tell her.

"I will tell you all God has told me we must do," Moses said as he settled slightly. "All those who wish to survive this final plague must take a year-old male lamb without spot or blemish into their home for four days.

"After that, on the fourteenth day, we must kill it but be careful to preserve its blood. Taking a branch of hyssop, everyone must dip into the bowl of lamb's blood and spread the blood on the side posts and on the lintel of the door. Then they must go inside the house marked with blood and roast the lamb whole and eat it in haste with unleavened bread. Whatever is left of the lamb is to be burned and not saved. While eating everyone must be girded and packed to flee as soon as the Lord gives us His sign."

"And what happens to those who do not obey?" Eliora asked, trying to follow along.

"The houses who do not follow these instructions will suffer the death of every first-born male in the house. Human and animal alike."

Puah's eyes watered again.

"We are to gather the lambs in the next few days."

She nodded as her mind filled with many thoughts. "There is much to prepare."

"Yes," he said. "But there is more."

"More?" She asked in fear.

"Good news," he tried to lighten his face into a smile. "All those who are foreigners in this land are invited to join in the protection of the Hebrew people. Any who wish to accept this invitation must join us in the homes of those who have covered their posts with the blood when we slaughter the lambs."

The faces of her Egyptian midwives flashed like lightning through Puah's mind. "Any foreigner?"

"All who obey are welcome to come with us."

She rushed toward the gate. "I have much to do."

She sent word with Eliora throughout the south for her Egyptian midwives to gather.

"Ladies," she called them to order. "I know I haven't been handling your training for some time, but I come before you now with a word."

"Go back to Goshen," one shouted from the crowd.

"Please listen to me."

"We've no need to hear any more from a Hebrew," another called.

"A plague," she tried again. "Another plague is coming. One that will be the worst of all plagues, but the one that Pharaoh will suffer to finally let the Hebrew people leave Egypt. I'm going with them and I-"

Many of them left without so much as a glance over their shoulders.

Layla stood in the empty space.

"Do you want to go with us?"

"Go where?"

The mentor thought for a moment. "I'm not really sure exactly where we are going, just that we are leaving Egypt. Moses says that everyone gets to choose, but if you don't come with us, there will be no leaving after that. The only protection from this last plague is to be in a house remarked with lamb's blood on the posts."

Layla sat down to think. "Do we have time to think the offer over?"

"Some. Not much."

As she turned to leave, Puah whispered a quick prayer for her. She knew first hand that following this God of her people wasn't easy.

Chapter 20

"In the tenth day of this month they shall take to them every man a lamb..."
-EXODUS 12:3

The tenth day of Nisan was upon them when Moses called for all Hebrews to meet him in the field between Memphis and the land of Goshen.

"Every man among you is to take for themselves a lamb according to the house of their fathers," he announced.

"One lamb for every house. If a household is too small to eat an entire lamb, then let him go to his neighbor's house and share together according to the number of people. The lamb you take shall be without blemish, a male of the first year out of the sheep or goats. You will keep the animal inside for the next four days. On the fourteenth day of this month, I will call you again together. There we will kill it in the evening for a meal."

"Where are we going to get a lamb and still keep up our work?" Eliora asked her mentor.

"You're welcome to join us," Miriam's voice sang over the dispersing crowd. "You two have pretty much become our extended family anyway."

"That's a generous offer."

"One we would love to accept," the older midwife agreed.

The next four days flew like a bird freed from his winter nest for Puah. Her heart grew heavy as she left each Egyptian home. Somewhere deep inside broke with the knowledge that she may never see their faces again. She and Eliora had helped deliver eight new babies and checked in on many women in Goshen as well.

They had finished their last stop just before evening when they came to Aaron's home.

"Greetings." Elisheba opened the gate wide. "I'm so glad Miriam invited you to have the Passover with us. Moses and Aaron will be returning shortly."

"Where are they?" Eliora wondered.

"In the valley." She sauntered toward the kitchen and picked up where she had left off. "They are helping slaughter the lambs for tonight."

"That's what all that distant commotion is."

"Can we give you a hand?" Puah offered.

The women worked as they waited for the brothers to return.

It wasn't long before the noise grew dim in the

fading light and Moses and Aaron finally returned home.

Aaron handed a bowl to his wife and kissed her cheek. "Hold on to this for a minute."

"Give me a hand," Moses ordered, slinging the dead lamb off his shoulder and onto the table.

The two men worked the stick through the animal and placed it over the waiting fire.

Miriam took over turning the spit so the meat would cook evenly.

A knock came at the door.

Moses and Aaron exchanged a glance.

"I'm not expecting anyone else." Aaron shrugged.

The younger brother went to see who stood on the other side of the gate.

"Does she belong to you?" Moses asked Puah when he returned.

Layla stood sheepishly behind him with two bags crossed over her body.

"She belongs to the Lord now."

"Tonight will be the night we all put our faith into action," Moses said.

He retrieved the bowl of blood from his sister-in-law and a hyssop branch from the table before stepping through the gate.

Dipping one end into the clay vessel, Moses used the branch to brush the crimson liquid onto the top of the doorpost and repeated the process to both sides of the doorway.

Puah watched the red liquid drip from the top post and resisted the shiver that fought its way up her back. It repeatedly dripped down into the sand staining the light color into a dark puddle. Blood hadn't bothered her since becoming a midwife. Seeing the animal blood spread across the entrance somehow seemed like something an Egyptian would do to combat a vengeful deity.

"Anything I can do to help?" She returned to Miriam's side.

"Go ask Moses what we should do next."

"Sure."

She went inside and found Aaron and Moses gathering everyone's supply bags into a pile. "What should I help with?"

"Such a great servant. Or are your typically busy hands feeling left out?" Aaron teased.

"I feel like I should be holding up my end of the gift of protection I've been given."

Moses' head popped up from his work. "If you see it has a gift, then why do you feel guilty enough to work for something that has been freely given?"

She thought about the question. "I don't have an answer."

Moses smiled to ease her tension. "Well, at least admitting that is a big step in wisdom. We appreciate a servant's heart, but do not think that your place here is dependent on the things you do for us."

"I understand."

"Good, now help us get these bags ready. Once our meal is over, we will need to be prepared to leave at a moment's notice."

Puah nodded and put her hands to work.

Miriam came in a little while later. "I believe the lamb is ready. Aaron, will you come help me bring it in?"

He nodded and followed her outside to the fire.

A few minutes later, Aaron brought the perfectly roasted lamb into the house.

"Everyone," Moses instructed the group. "Get your bags on and come around the food."

Once everyone had prepared themselves and gathered, Moses gave further directions, "Aaron, grab your staff and please hand me mine."

The brother complied.

"Right, now let us thank God. Lord, thank You for this meal and for Your ultimate protection," he prayed. "We have been obedient to Your commands and thank You for leading us. Let us be sensitive to the moment You call us to leave. Thank You for moving us out of Egypt into the land You have promised our father Abraham. Now, be with us, Lord as we eat and strengthen our bodies to follow Your leading." Then he passed around the unleavened bread and made sure everyone had a handful of bitter herbs to eat with their meat just as God had instructed.

The group of people ate in silence as the

weight of uncertainty of what lay ahead began to sink into their thoughts.

After everyone had their fill of meat and bread, Moses spoke, "Miriam, please take all the leftover parts and place them in the fire. There is to be nothing left."

Miriam nodded, gathered the picked through bones, and threw them onto the smoldering fire. "What next?" she asked, rejoining the group.

"Now, we wait. We shall stay alert and prepared for the sign from the Lord."

As it grew darker outside, Puah's shoulders started to burn with the weight of her bags. Then a strange quietness came over the city of Avaris.

She looked around the room and met Eliora's eyes.

"There is no sound out there," her apprentice whispered. "Not even a stray dog barking,"

She nodded and set her attention out the open window to watch for signs of movement or the slightest sound.

A strong wind blew through the street and when the night grew to its darkest, a deafening sound startled them.

Puah rose to her feet along with the rest of them. Each had to place their hands over their ears to keep out the noise.

"What is that?" Eliora screamed to be heard over the roar.

The mentor knew the sound in her heart, but

never in her life had she heard the sheer magnitude as in that moment. "It's the sound of a mother's cry."

"Mothers," Moses corrected. "The unified cry of all mothers who have just discovered their firstborn sons dead in their beds."

Tears welled up in Puah's eyes. Her tender heart broke as she remembered the faces of each and every Egyptian baby. Her mind flashed with the twisted faces of agony of all the women she had helped bring their little ones into the world. Those innocent children had suffered death in that moment because their parents had not obeyed the word of the Lord.

Though the palace was quite a long distance from them, she could hear the cries of Queen Satiah in her mind who no doubt was laying with Amenemhat. With all the tension hanging in the air, her cries were mixed in the multitude after she discovered his cold body and wailed for him. God had promised that not even the house of Pharaoh would escape this plague.

"Is that our sign?" Eliora's voice brought Puah back to the moment.

Moses shook his head and looked over at the sobbing midwife. "Steady."

She looked up and nodded as she wiped away the tears from her cheeks and adjusted the bag on her shoulder.

Aaron was whispering a prayer when Moses

suddenly stood.

"It's time," he commanded sternly.

"Time to leave?" Miriam asked.

Moses nodded. "But one more thing to do before we leave."

Chapter 21

"Speak now in the ears of the people, and let every man borrow of his neighbour, and every woman of her neighbour, jewels of silver, and jewels of gold."
-EXODUS 11:2

The two midwives followed Miriam and her sister-in-law out into the night and to the valley that separated the land of Goshen from the rest of Egypt. Moses and Aaron had sent word for the people to gather.

"God has given a command." He stood on a large pile of rocks so that his voice could carry over the crowd. "Go into the cities to the south and borrow from our Egyptian neighbors. Take from them jewels of silver and gold and clothes. Anything they are willing to offer to you, take and pack among your belongings."

"He's serious?" Eliora asked.

"Seems like it. Let's grab some bags and get to work."

"It's a good thing our midwives are experts at collecting by now."

Once the two had gathered every spare bag they could from their home, they started knocking on their neighbor's doors.

When the servants opened, Puah asked, "We're seeking provisions."

"Here," they would say shoving handfuls of precious jewels and garments at them before swiftly shutting the door.

Women and men crisscrossed down the street knocking on every Egyptian gate. Each held out an open bag to be filled with anything the family had to offer.

"Leave us," the Egyptian at the next house told Puah after handing her a pile of clean linens. "If you stay any longer, we will all be dead."

She lifted the heavy satchel over her head and allowed it to hang across her body.

Meeting Eliora in the middle of the street, the two rounded a corner and were faced with one last house.

"Oh no," the younger woman gasped. "How can we go there?"

Puah stared at the freshly painted white limestone with tears in her eyes. No blood stained the post of the door. "I don't know if I can."

"Maybe we should just leave. No one will know that we didn't ask."

"God will." She walked toward the house and

knocked.

When no answer came, she tried again.

The door swung open wide.

"You!" Sofh stood clinging to the doorframe. "How dare you show your faces here."

"We've come to-"

"I know exactly what you've come for," she roared. "You think I'm just going to hand over my possessions to your kind? You've already taken my son." She sank to the sand. "My beautiful son." She wept. "You took him from me."

"We didn't take your child." Puah's own eyes watered. "We helped bring him into the world."

The woman looked up at them. "Take it all." She waved into the house. "I don't care anymore. It all means nothing now." She pulled her knees up to her chest to give them a pathway and buried her face into her robe.

"What do we do?" Eliora whispered.

"Gather whatever supplies we're lacking. I'll stay here with her."

The student stepped over the weeping woman and entered the house.

Puah knelt beside Sofh and put her arm around her. "God of the universe," she prayed aloud. "Be with this grieving mother. Send her comfort and provision in her time of need."

The woman's sobs increased to loud wailing.

"I don't personally know the depths of her sorrow, but I know You do."

JENIFER JENNINGS

"Ready?" Eliora said, returning from inside.

Puah nodded and stood. "I'm sorry for your loss. I can only hope that you'll one day see our God for who He truly is."

"He is a murderer and a coward." She rose on her unsteady feet. "Now get out of my sight."

The door slammed hard between them.

"Well that was interesting," the younger woman attempted to lighten the mood. "Whose home do we bring a little more sorrow to next?"

"Let's go see Queen Satiah. Surely she will have lots to offer us."

"You're the mentor." The apprentice effortlessly swung her crammed bag over her shoulder.

As they searched the rooms of the palace for its queen, they met Moses standing inside a hall facing the throne room.

"Moses?"

He turned to them.

Puah saw the dark bags under his eyes from lack of sleep. She'd seen the same look on more than one new mother's face. Tired. Drained. Worn out.

"What are you doing here?" she questioned him. "What about Pharaoh's order to have you killed if you showed your face again?"

"One more request left."

"He's agreed that all of us, including our herds, could leave. What could possibly be so important

256

as to risk your neck?"

"A promise, dear midwife." He stepped into the room.

Puah followed with her student close on her heels.

"I thought I told you to take your people and leave," Pharaoh barked from his golden throne.

"We are in the process even now of moving our people out of your land."

"Then why do you stand before me?"

"There is one more thing I require," Moses said, his firm words flowing like honey from his lips. It had taken almost the entire five months for the Egyptian language to return to his mind, but he spoke it proudly now.

"Haven't you taken enough from us?" Pharaoh narrowed his eyes.

"One last thing."

The royal man waited.

"I want the bones of Joseph."

"Who's Joseph?"

"Someone your people have forgotten. He was the eleventh son of Jacob. Sold into Egyptian slavery, he interpreted dreams of Pharaoh Senusret III and gave warning of a coming drought. For this, Pharaoh bestowed upon him many titles and placed him as Vizier, second in command only to himself. For this, your people welcomed my people into your land and we lived in peace.

"For many generations, Hebrews and Egyptians worked beside each other. Until Pharaoh Amenhotep I came to rule," his recounting of Egyptian history mixed with his own people's stories streamed together like currents in the Nile. "After finally overthrowing the previously ruling Hyksos and removing them from Egypt, Pharaoh Amenhotep I's power gave rise to a new dynasty. One that forgot about Joseph. One that began to fear the Hebrews as enemies instead of equals. He began to slowly place taskmasters over the Hebrews. Each of his successors increased our burdens and made us slaves until you took the throne."

Pharaoh's chest heaved. His cheeks burned red.

"Our God has hardened your heart to display His power," Moses continued. "Now, our people will be free and I am here to keep the last command given by Joseph. When we leave this land and return to our own, we are to take his bones with us."

"Is this true?" Pharaoh grunted at his aide.

The short man rushed off to find the answer.

Pharaoh Thutmose III and Moses both stared at each other in the silence. One stewing in blatant hatred. The other standing in power.

Moments later, the aid returned with an unrolled scroll. "It seems there is a palace complex built in Goshen. It has a villa and a garden containing a small pyramid tomb. In it lays the sarcophagus of a Vizier. A man named Zaphnath-Paaneah."

"Formerly, a Hebrew named Joseph. If you had given more focus to your studies, brother, you would have remembered."

"You realize," Pharaoh countered. "If you remove his body from its place of rest, you will be destroying his journey to the afterlife and the protection we have placed on his tomb."

"I do."

"Very well. You may take the body. I don't need even one Hebrew left in my land." He paused after spitting out each word like daggers. "But you must remove it yourself. Not too difficult a task for slaves."

Moses bowed his head slightly before leaving.

Hours later, Puah walked with Moses, Aaron, and Miriam to the large villa.

"This place is magnificent," she remarked. "It's like a perfect blend of Egyptian and Hebrew styles."

If only people could meld together as easily as it seems the two styles blended.

"I remember coming here as a boy," Aaron said. "Mother pointed out that the twelve columns there stood for each of the twelve sons of Jacob." He pointed to each one. "And the two apartments at the front here were for Jacob's sons, Ephraim and Manasseh." He spread his arms wide as they passed through the main entrance. On either side of the group stood entrances into other parts of the villa.

"I loved when she told the stories of Joseph," Miriam said. "I could always imagine him here."

They walked through the rest of the villa and out the back where they were greeted by a large garden. Trees swayed in the gentle breeze and wonderful scents of fresh blossoms filled the air.

On another day, the picturesque view would have brought peace to Puah. Today, it brought heartache as she was preparing to leave her home, her Egyptian patients, and everything she had ever known.

When they made their way deeper into the garden, they found a group of Hebrew men hard at work meticulously removing each brick from its place. The small pyramid in front of them stood proudly Egyptian but inside held the body of one of their own and they were there to keep a promise.

"We're almost through," one of the men reported to Moses. He wiped his forehead with the back of his hand.

Moses nodded.

The man ducked back inside the opening.

"I've always wanted a garden like this." Miriam closed her eyes and inhaled deeply the sweet scent of daisies and cornflowers.

Puah could see Miriam's body relax. If only she

could let her guard down as easily. Pharaoh had already changed his mind several times. It wouldn't surprise her if he stopped them once again.

Her heart twisted. She was broken over the loss of innocent life in the middle of this power struggle. Many of those lives she had welcomed into the world. Her touch had been their first experience outside of their mother's womb. Egyptian or Hebrew. It didn't matter to her. Babies were precious. Life was precious.

She hadn't wanted to visit their mothers after the last plague. She didn't want to look into their empty eyes and ask them for treasures. To them, she had been one of the ones who had taken their most valued treasure. When truly, she had been one to bring life, not destroy it.

"We're in!" A shout echoed from the opening.

Moses and Aaron bent quickly inside.

Puah waved Miriam to go ahead.

"No. I think I'm going to stay out here." She wrapped her arms around herself and took another deep breath. "I want to enjoy this for as long as I can."

Puah nodded and ducked her head into the entrance.

It was dark. She moved slowly down the steps to let her eyes adjust. By the time she reached the room housing the tomb at the bottom, she could see the torches of the workers.

Moses and Aaron stood on either side of the sarcophagus and the few men pushed themselves against the walls.

All were staring at the carved gold-plated face of Joseph.

"It's time," Moses whispered.

The men stepped forward and lifted the body-shaped box out of the tomb. The two brothers followed closely behind.

Puah stood in the empty tomb examining all the jars and treasures of Egyptian life. Though she had never experienced it for herself, she had served close enough to witness all the luxuries of royal life.

One item caught her attention and she made her way over to it. A statue stood proudly displayed. It was carved in the shape of an Egyptian man, but it was decorated much differently. The arms were crossed in the typical Egyptian style. Everything else about him was clearly Hebrew. His hair was red and styled the way a Hebrew man would wear his and not at all in the fashion of a black Egyptian wig.

Instead of the sun-baked skin of an Egyptian man, the skin was painted yellow. Most of all, the outer garment was not of the golds and blues of Egyptian, but red and black like a Hebrew garment. Like a coat. A coat of many colors.

She smiled, remembering the story her mother used to tell.

"Staying?" Moses asked from the bottom step.
"Just looking."

He entered the room and stood beside her.

"What's that in his hand?" She pointed to the short stick in the statue's hand.

"A throw-stick. Their way to mark him as a foreigner. Though he was highly respected for what he did to save Egypt, they wanted to remind everyone that he still wasn't an Egyptian." He sighed. "We need to get going."

"Of course."

"Be quick." He turned and left up the stairs.

She reached up and grazed the face of the statue with her fingertips. "I know you knew we'd be leaving someday, but I never thought it would be in my lifetime. I know I should be happy to leave, but I was happy serving here." She bowed her head. "God, give me strength like Joseph to go where you've called me to go."

She took one last gaze toward the statue and exited the tomb.

Chapter 22

*"And the LORD went before them by day in a
pillar of a cloud, to lead them the way; and by
night in a pillar of fire, to give them light; to go
by day and night:"*
-EXODUS 13:21

The midwives gathered together in their place in
the extensive group which had gathered by tribes
in Rameses.

Moses stood ahead of them, staring into the
waiting wilderness.

Puah shared a glance with Eliora who
shrugged her shoulders.

Out of the clear sky, a cloud column gathered
before them.

"What's that?" Layla pointed.

"A sandstorm?" the mentor offered. "They are
quite common out here in the desert."

"Then why does it look like a pillar?"

"I don't know."

"Who's that?" Eliora gestured with her head.

The midwife stood on her toes to see over the crowd.

A man standing in a white robe shone before them.

"Do not be alarmed," Moses' voice boomed. "They are from the Lord and are here to guide us."

The man and the pillar moved forward and he followed them.

"Ready?" Eliora called over her shoulder.

"As I'll ever be," Puah answered back. She turned to the woman beside her. "Are you?

"No." Layla swallowed hard. "But I guess there is no more time for indecision."

The people journeyed from Rameses to Succoth. They only stopped briefly to collect the men who had been working in the mines before moving on to Etham.

Once they reached the open area away from the last city, Puah removed the bags from her body and set them down. She stretched out her back and called to her guild, "Everyone doing well?"

Nods of approval and slight smiles flashed at her.

"Remember when Moses drove all the locusts into the sea?" Eliora waved toward the water.

"I do."

"I would wager the fish ate well that night." She laughed.

The midwives talked with excitement about all

that lay ahead of them as they ate unleavened bread.

"I don't know if I can get used to this." Eliora tore off another piece and placed it on her tongue.

"It won't be too long before we reach Canaan." Puah chewed the bite in her mouth. "Think of settling down in a new house. Maybe we'll be favored to find a larger one and bring on more apprentices."

The younger woman dipped her head. "You're ready to get rid of me that quickly?"

"I mean to make you a mentor in the new land."

"Really?" She lifted her head to reveal a wide smile.

"I think you're about ready to take on your own students."

The girl wrapped her arms around her mentor. "Thank you."

As the sun dipped behind them, the cloud column transformed into a bright pillar of flames.

Gasps filled the air.

"Fear not," Moses explained. "This is again the Lord's provision for us."

"Well, it'll certainly keep wild animals away," Eliora stated.

"That thing will keep anything away," Layla added.

"Get some sleep, ladies," the mentor called. "We still have a long journey ahead of us."

Puah and Eliora settled on the ground with a bag under their heads for a pillow.

"We're just supposed to lay down here?" Layla protested. "In the dirt? Like dogs?"

"Get used to it," the mentor said.

"It's entertaining following our God, huh?" Eliora teased.

"Oh, such fun." Layla dropped her bag on the ground and sat with a thud. She pulled her knees up to her chest. "I miss home already."

"Sleep," Puah suggested. "Things will look different in the morning."

Once the sun rose, the mentor woke her sleeping students. "Time to start walking again."

"Can we have breakfast first?" Layla asked, rubbing her eyes.

"Here," Eliora tossed a small bundle toward her. "I saved some dried figs and flatbread from last night."

The guild of women joined the enormous crowd of Hebrews as they marched onward.

When they encamped again, it was at Pihahiroth between Migdol and the sea.

"Those mountains are beautiful," Eliora remarked.

"I'm thankful we aren't planning on climbing them," Layla mocked. "Are we?"

The old midwife laughed. "We'll follow wherever that cloud leads."

Late into the day, the sound of thunderings

from behind them caused Puah to turn.

"A storm?" Eliora asked.

"It sounds too close to the ground," Layla offered.

The old midwife's eyes widened. "Chariots! I'd know that sound anywhere."

When the people looked, they saw hundreds of Egypt's finest warriors heading straight for them. Each chariot held one driver and one Egyptian soldier. The fighters were armed with bows and trained to achieve incredible accuracy on their stable platform. Inside the basket was room for additional arrows and short spears to use when the arrows ran out or for a close-range battle.

Panic gripped the hearts of the Hebrews.

"Did you lead us out here to die?" a man cried out.

"We're trapped between the mountains and the sea," a woman wept.

"Moses led us south when we should have traveled north." An older man demanded.

"This is all his fault," another woman blamed.

"No one asked you to free us from under the Egyptians," the first man pierced.

Murmurings and pleas raced through the group like lightning.

"It would have been better for us to stay there serving than to die out here."

"Were there not enough graves in Egypt that we had to come out here to be buried?"

Many tried to flee from the approaching soldiers, but with nowhere to run they only ended up running in circles.

"Don't be afraid!" Moses shouted over the people. "Stand still and you will see the salvation of the Lord today. Take a good look at the Egyptians you see coming for us. You will not look on their faces again. The Lord will fight for you as you hold still."

The peculiar man who had been leading the way vanished from before them and reappeared behind them. The column of cloud followed after him and spread out to the rear of the people. It grew so dark, they could not see through it.

"Do you think that will stop them?" Eliora asked, tightening her grip on Puah's arm.

She could still hear the sound of horses whinnying in the distance. Wheels roared toward them and men shouted from behind the veil. "I hope so."

Moses walked close to the water's edge and held up his staff. He stretched his arms over the sea.

A mighty east wind kicked up and caused the waters to stir.

"Look," Puah pointed.

To the amazed disbelief of everyone present, the wind was pushing the water in front of Moses away to form a route through the sea.

As the water divided, he cried out, "Go!"

Puah didn't hesitate. She began running toward the path of freedom.

The guild of women gave chase and overtook her.

Her legs burned, but she didn't slow. When her bare feet hit the sands, she slid to a halt. She wiggled her toes in the dry seafloor. "It's firm!"

People shoved passed her.

She stayed in the back of the group and stared at the two walls of water on either side of her as she walked. "Wow!" she gasped. "It's like glass."

With a last glance over her shoulder, she saw the chariots rush through the cloud heading straight for her.

"Go!" Moses ordered.

She lifted the hem of her dress to give her legs more room to run.

Moses was the last to cross through the waters just as the morning rays shone over the horizon. He stretched his hand over the water again and caused them to return to their place.

Puah searched the sea as it rushed together. Not a single Egyptian warrior remained in the flood.

"Where did they all go?" Eliora asked. "They were right behind us."

She held her hands up to her open mouth. "I don't know."

"I will sing unto the Lord for He has triumphed gloriously," Moses' voice bellowed out.

"He has thrown the horse and rider into the sea. The Lord is my strength and song."

They turned to him.

"He is my salvation! He is my God! I will build him a dwelling place and I will exalt Him.

"The Lord is a man of war," Aaron joined in. "The Lord is His name. Pharaoh's chariots and all his army were thrown into the sea to drown."

"The depths have covered them as they sank to the bottom like stones," Moses added. "Your right hand, God, is mighty with power. Your right hand, God, has dashed our enemy into pieces."

"Your wrath has consumed them like stubble," another man sang along.

"With a blast of Your nostrils." Moses lifted his face to the sky. "The waters were gathered together and stood upright in form. The enemy said, 'I will pursue and overtake them to spoil.' But You, Lord, blew the wind and made the sea cover them."

"Who is like the Lord among their gods?" Aaron danced. "Who is like the Lord, who is glorious in holiness, fearful in praises, and does amazing wonders?"

"None!" a group of men shouted out.

"In Your mercy, Lord, You have led and redeemed Your people. You have guided them with Your strength." Moses stood on a large boulder. "The people will hear and be afraid. Sorrow will take hold over this land." He waved his arms around. "The Dukes of Edom will be amazed. The mighty men of Moab will tremble. All the inhabitants of Canaan will melt away."

Shouts came from all over the camp.

"Fear and dread shall come upon them all," he continued. "The Lord will bring His purchased people into the land and plant them there to fulfill the promise He made. The Lord shall reign forever and ever."

Another round of praise broke out all over.

Miriam took a timbrel and began to dance.

Other women took up their timbrels and followed after her.

"Sing to the Lord," she chanted. "For He has been gloriously victorious. The horse and his rider have been cast into the sea."

Puah and her midwives joined Miriam and the others.

The people sang and danced in front of the cloud column until it transformed once again into a pillar of fire under the star-filled sky.

Chapter 23

"And it came to pass, because the midwives feared God, that he made them houses."
-EXODUS 1:21

A few days later, they made it to Marah to camp. Before the midwife guild could finish setting up their own tent, they had been called to duty.

Batya paced the sands of her tent, rubbing her huge belly.

"How often?" Puah asked, watching the mother walk.

"It's been like this all day," she groaned. "Oww..."

"That's a good sign. If the pains are coming more often, then the baby will be here soon."

"How long?"

She rolled up her sleeves. "Whenever the baby decides to come." She chuckled. "My apprentice should be back any moment and then we'll take a look at you."

Eliora dashed into the tent. "You called?"

"Ah, here she is."

"I've got enough clean linens for twins."

"God forbid." Batya held her stomach tight.

The women laughed.

"Let's get you set up to meet this little one," the mentor said.

After hours of difficult pushing, Batya rested on the arms of two midwives. "I just don't know how much longer I can keep this up."

"Not much longer now," Puah informed her. "The baby's head is nearly there." She motioned Eliora over with her chin.

The woman obeyed.

"Hold her leg there while I adjust her," she instructed.

The apprentice huddled down to help.

"There we are. Baby is coming now. Almost-"

A strong cry interrupted her.

"A girl!" Eliora shouted.

Batya fell back in relief.

"There, there, little one," the older midwife comforted. "We've got you." She wiped the baby clean before laying her on Betya's chest.

"Have you and Zelophehad discussed a name?"

"Yes." She rubbed the dark hair of the little girl. "Mahlah."

"You did a great job with that one," Puah complimented Eliora as they slowly walked back toward their tent.

"I love to help bring babies into the world."

After they finished hammering the tent pegs into the ground, the two midwives quickly set up a few comforts.

Puah grabbed two large shoulder bags. "Will you accompany me to my next meeting?"

"Of course, who is it with?"

"Moses."

"You have a meeting with Moses?"

She nodded and patted the large bag hanging over her shoulder. "I have something for him."

"I see." She looked down to her feet. "Do you think Hoshea will be there?"

"He has taken the young soldier under his wing recently. It wouldn't surprise me." She grinned at how speaking of the warrior made her apprentice's face shift colors. "There is something I'd like to discuss with you as we walk as well."

They ducked out of the tent and into the open sands.

"Speak on," Eliora offered.

"I'm happy to finally see our people free, though I feel my sight might be limited."

"What does that mean?"

"In short, I believe I won't get to see the promised land with the rest of you. At least, maybe not enjoy much of it."

"Don't speak this way."

"I speak truth."

Eliora's eyes watered. "I refuse to think on it."

"I need you to lead the midwives."

"Me?"

"I've watched you grow from that uncertain young lady into a well-educated midwife. There is no one else I'd rather see teach the young ones about our work."

"I do teach them. I've already started with the two apprentices you lined up for me."

"I know, but what I'm asking is for you to take on all my responsibilities. See over the training of the teams and mentors. Be the one they call with the difficulties."

She shook her head.

"Do this old woman's heart a favor and just accept my offer. It would bring me great peace."

"For you, then yes."

"Ladies, it is wonderful to see you again," Miriam welcomed the women just outside her tent. "Moses has been expecting you."

The two bowed and stepped inside.

"I was excited to hear of your request to see us."

"As was I," Moses said, coming in from the other side of the curtain followed by Aaron and Hoshea.

Puah greeted the men. "I'm grateful that you accepted my request."

"Of course." He waved toward the pillows.

Eliora chose instead to stand off to the side behind her mentor.

"How could I turn away one of the women

who helped protect me and so many others?" Moses continued as he sat with the men.

Puah settled into the soft fabric beside Miriam. "That was so long ago."

"But not forgotten," he corrected. "Now, what is it you've come to speak about?"

"This." She raised the straps over her head and handed the bags to him.

"I don't understand."

"During our time in Egypt, I never delivered anything other than a healthy baby to a Hebrew. Only God's power could keep our humble people alive when the richest kingdom in the world can't keep their babies from dying. Even with their choice food and luxurious lifestyles." She pointed to the stuffed bag.

"Those are the records of all the births during Egypt. They have been passed down from mentor to apprentice. My mentor gave them to me, but I feel as though they need to be given over to you in order to be kept safe. My time is growing short and I wanted to get them to you before it was too late."

"I will take good care of these." He pressed the bags to his chest.

"Then I'll leave in peace." She started to rise.

"Before you go." He waved her back down. "May I show you something?"

"Of course."

Moses rose and stepped behind one of the veils

dividing the tent into rooms and retrieved a parchment. He brought it to her and unrolled it on the ground. "I have a document of my own to show you." He pointed to a place in the writing.

Puah read over the words scribed on the scroll. *The king of Egypt said to the Hebrew midwives, whose names were Shiphrah and Puah...*

Tears formed at the corners of her eyes at the beloved name of her mentor. "What's this?"

"It's a record. God has impressed on me to write and instructed me to include your story."

"Oh my." Her fingers grazed over the parchment. "Thank you."

"Shiphrah would have been proud of you," Moses said as he rolled up the scroll.

"She would have been more proud of you," Puah praised him. "You've led our people to freedom."

"God led our people to freedom. He simply used me to accomplish it."

She smiled wide. "Perhaps He used us each in our own way."

Want to find out what happens next?

Miriam is finally free. Will she make it to the promised land?

With Egypt behind them, Miriam and the other Hebrews are finally heading to the land of promise. A land following with milk and honey.

When grumbles and complaints break out like a plague among the people, Miriam is no exception. Her brother, Aaron, leads the priests while their youngest brother, Moses, leads the people. What's Miriam to do? God speaks in her dreams and gives her songs of praise and prophecy, but she longs for more.

Discontented with Moses' leadership, the people choose a new leader to head back to the familiar land of Egypt. God doesn't want them to return to slavery, but being the chivalrous God He is, He won't force them into His offer of peace and blessings. Instead, He gives them exactly what they want.

Will Miriam make it out of the wilderness or will she be forced to wander just out of reach of the promised destination? Follow Miriam's gripping journey of faith in Book 2 of the Faith Finders Series, "Wilderness Wanderer."

Also by Jenifer Jennings

Special Collections and Boxed Sets
Biblical Historical stories from the Old Testament to the New, these special boxed editions offer a great way to catch up or to fall in love with Jenifer Jennings' books for the first time.

Faith Finder Series: Books 1-3
Faith Finders Series: Books 4-6
The Rebekah Series: Books 1-3

* * *

Faith Finders Series:
Go deeper into the stories of these familiar faith heroines.

Midwives of Moses
Wilderness Wanderer
Crimson Cord
A Stolen Wife
At His Feet
Lasting Legacy

* * *

The Rebekah Series:

Follow Rebekah on her faith journey through life.

The Stranger
The Journey
The Hope

* * *

Servant Siblings Series:

*They were Jesus' siblings,
but they become His followers.*

James
Joseph
Assia
Jude
Lydia
Simon
Salome

Find all of these titles at your favorite retailer or at:
jeniferjennings.com/books

Thank You!

Hubby, I love you more than you'll ever know. Without you, none of this would be possible.

Kids, you're both too young to fully understand, but I do this for you. My goal is always to show Jesus and this is what He has created me to do.

Word Weavers Clay County, you know you're all awesome. I'm just glad God directed me to our group to remind each of you of that fact.

Jenifer's Jewels, thank you for being so responsive to the first peeks of this story. I enjoyed each of your feedbacks. You each make the team so wonderful.

Betas: Audrey and Deb, you gals were amazing. Thanks for all your hard work.

My readers, I want to thank you. If I could, I'd travel around shaking the hands of everyone who picks up a copy of my work. Enjoying the product of someone's passion and sacrifice is no small act. I'm truly grateful I get to write and share my heart with all of you.